THE
POWER
OF
HARMONY

THE POWER OF HARMONY

Jan L. Coates

Red Deer Press

Published in Canada by Red Deer Press
195 Allstate Parkway, Markham, ON, L3R 4T8

www.reddeerpress.com

Published in the United States by Red Deer Press
311 Washington Street, Brighton, Massachusetts, 02135

Edited for the Press by Peter Carver
Cover and text design by Daniel Choi
Cover image courtesy of Masterfile and iStock

We acknowledge with thanks the Canada Council for the Arts, and the Ontario Arts Council for their support of our publishing program. We acknowledge the financial support of the Government of Canada through the Canada Book Fund (CBF) for our publishing activities.

Library and Archives Canada Cataloguing in Publication
Coates, Jan, 1960-
    The power of harmony / Jan Coates.
ISBN 978-0-88995-495-3
    I. Title.
PS8605.O238P69 2013   jC813'.6   C2013-901672-4

Publisher Cataloging-in-Publication Data (U.S)
Coates, Jan.
    Power of harmony / Jan Coates.
[264] p. : cm.
Summary: Set during the late 1960s in the town of Springhill, Nova Scotia—famed for its coal-mining disasters and for being the birthplace of Anne Murray—the story is about a young girl whose new best friend is a First Nations girl recently arrived from a nearby residential school that has shut down, who is being verbally abused and bullied by her new classmates. It's a tale of overcoming social and racial barriers, finding new friends, and the power of music.
ISBN-13: 978-0-88995-495-3 (pbk.)
1. Bullying – Juvenile fiction. 3. Friendship in adolescence – Juvenile fiction. I. Title
[Fic] dc23   PZ7.C63847Po 2013

Printed and bound in Canada

This book is a work of fiction. References to real people, events, organizations, or locales are intended only to provide a sense of authenticity and are used to advance the fictional narrative. All other characters, and all incidents and dialogue, are drawn from the author's imagination and are not to be construed as real. The opinions expressed by some characters in the book are in no way those of the author (or publisher) but are representative of attitudes of the time.

For my big sister, Nance, who knows (almost)
all my stories;
my baby sister, Carol Beth, whose voice
we never got to hear ...
and
for all the silent watchers,
struggling to find their voices—be brave.

While with an eye made quiet by the power
Of harmony, and the deep power of joy,
We see into the life of things.
—William Wordsworth

CHAPTER 1

(WHEREIN The Voice of an Angel Faints)

The mirror on the back of the bathroom door's all cloudy. Makes me look like an angel. A skinny, freckly angel in an itchy white dress. I've got the voice of an angel, too. That's what my music teacher tells me. Only I don't want to be in God's heavenly choir. Not yet. Since that's just a nice way of saying somebody died.

I pull up my knee socks, then wet my fingers to flatten the cowlick in my bangs. Fold my hands together in front of my belly and whisper-sing. But I look so silly with my eyebrows wiggling up and down and my mouth all popped open that I burst out laughing. The kind of laughing that might melt into crying.

Dad's waiting for me in the church hallway, leaning back against the wall on two legs of his chair, right next to a pink and green poster. Whistling, acting like everything's hunky-dory. "All set?"

I try to smile, but after the bathroom door clicks closed behind me, it's quiet. Too quiet. I read the poster. Twice. *Cumberland County Music Festival, 1968. Spring Into Song!* All of a sudden, the people inside the main part of the church start clapping. I squeeze my belly, try to settle the butterflies. "How many people are in there? I thought there'd just be a few."

Dad shrugs, pats me on the head, then walks over to the desk and tells the lady my name. She leans over so she can see me hiding behind him. "There are only ten girls in your class, dear." She smiles, but it's the kind of smile that says she wouldn't be in my shoes for all the tea in China. "You're number three on the list. Did you bring your music?"

Only ten girls! My music? Nobody told me to bring my music.

> *Come take up your Hats, and away let us haste*
> *To the Butterfly's Ball, and the Grasshopper's Feast.*
> *The Trumpeter, Gad-fly, has summon'd the Crew,*
> *And the Revels are now only waiting for you.*

"Her music teacher, Althea Dill, should be here any minute," Dad says.

Why didn't I bring my copy of the music? What'll I do if I forget my words? Or if I need to pee again? My fingers creep up into my mouth, and my bad eye twitches where Junior

Tattrie binged me with a rock last year after I beat him in a race. Still slams shut when I get in a tizzy.

The big wooden doors swing open and a bunch of little girls giggle out into the hallway. At least none of them's crying.

"You can sit in the front row, dear," the desk lady says. "The seats are numbered, and you're to sit in chair number three."

Dad squeezes my hand, then I walk up the long aisle, alone, keeping my eyes straight ahead on a round stained-glass window. It's a girl angel, standing on some rocks with a bird on her hand. She's got curly red hair, like Bethy's. Only longer.

The tapping of my Sunday-school shoes echoes off the high wooden ceiling. *The lips, the teeth, the tip of the tongue* ... I'm the first one there, so I sit down in seat number three, in front of the place where the minister's supposed to stand. I wiggle around a little, straighten out my dress, then cross my ankles together under my chair and sit on my hands. I stare up at the angel and the shiny gold organ pipes. Pull my right hand out and cram all four fingertips into my mouth.

"I'm so nervous!" I jerk my fingers back out when Sarah Saunders parks herself in the seat next to mine. Number two. "Aren't you?"

I try to smile at her but there's something wrong with my lips. They're frozen and I'm having trouble breathing. What's *she* doing here? I manage to jerk my head up and down, like a chicken.

"I decided to come at the last minute," Sarah says. "My Mother got me in."

The rest of the seats fill up fast, but I don't know any of the other girls. I peek over my shoulder and search for Miss Dill in the audience. Dad nods and gives me a wink.

"Saw Dill Pickle in the hall—talking to the adjudicator," Sarah says. "Likely telling him how good my voice is." She flips her blonde hair back, then looks my dress up and down. Frowns at the polka-dot ruffle that's trying to strangle me. "I like your dress—hand-me-down from your cousin?"

I nod.

"You like mine? I got it at Margolian's on the weekend. It's the latest style in New York City, just like in the magazines."

My fingers crawl back up into my mouth. I look sideways at her orange and green dress. Tangerine orange and lime green. Except for the colors, looks to me like most of the plaid school jumpers hanging in my closet at home. I'm pretty sure they didn't come from New York City.

A light flashes somewhere to my left. We all look over and a man takes our picture. "Big smiles for *The Record*, girls," he says. "Say cheese!" Too late, I remember my mouth's full of fingers.

The desk lady gets up and announces, "Class Number 1065, Girls Vocal Solo, Ten Years and Under."

Another lady, wearing a gray dress and a pearl necklace, walks up the little stairs and sits down on the piano bench and fiddles with the handle to make it higher. The girl sitting in chair number one gets up, straightens her poofy pink dress, and follows her. I chew on my fingers, watch, and listen. The piano's going too fast, and she's racing to keep up. Plus I can't hardly hear her because she's whispering. Or maybe it's because my heart's beating so loud.

She curtsies and everybody claps. Then Miss Dill goes up and sits down at the piano. She's wearing her concert outfit: a straight black skirt with a crisp white blouse and the sparkly treble-clef brooch I gave her last year. She's not old but she's got gray hair, all tied up in a big knot on top of her head.

Sarah prances up the stairs and across the floor, then clears her throat a couple of times. I clear mine, too. She glares down at me, then turns to the piano and gives Miss Dill a Queen nod. Miss Dill starts playing at just the right speed, not too fast, not too slow. Sarah still sounds like a crow. Does something chickeny with her neck when she sings—seems like she's hauling her words up out of a coal mine in some creaky old cart. Everybody claps anyway.

Then it's my turn. Miss Dill stays at the piano and smiles out at me. She looks small and far away, and there's a fuzzy circle all around her and the piano. I clear my dry throat and swallow a bunch of times. Sarah sits back down beside me. I blink, stand up, tug on my dress, and try to tuck my hair behind my ears, which isn't that easy with a pixie cut.

But there's something wrong with my skinny stick legs.

They've turned into logs.

I close my eyes and try to move one foot, then the other one. Like some kind of robot. When my toe bumps into the stairs, I open my eyes, grab onto the railing, and pull myself up. The shiny wooden floor's enormous. The middle of it looks a hundred miles away.

When I finally get there, I stare down at my shoes for a few seconds, then look out. At all the pews. All the faces. The gawking eyes. My brain freezes up. My face gets hot and itchy, like an infected boil about to explode. I try to fold my hands together in front of my belly, but they're shaking so bad they can't find each other in the air. I grab onto the sides of my dress instead and hold on tight.

And then I look at Sarah.

Fixing her hair and giving me her smirkle: part smile, mostly smirk.

The whole room begins bouncing, makes my belly woozy, turns my log legs to Jell-O. When I close my eyes, try to suck in some air, the floor flies up. Smacks me right in the forehead. *H-o-o-omerrrun!* Fireflies flash inside my eyelids. My teeth taste bloody.

"Gracious me! Are you all right, Jennifer?" Miss Dill waves her music around. The breeze feels nice on my cheek. I smile, close my eyes again, and start to sing.

> *The Trumpeter, Gad-fly, has summon'd the Crew,*
> *And the Revels are now only waiting for ...*

CHAPTER 2

(WHEREIN The Voice of an Angel Recovers)

M e! My eyes pop open. The Music Festival! I roll over onto my back and look up, way up, at the wooden ceiling and the upside down angel. Miss Dill, Dad, and the desk lady are all staring down at me.

"You okay, Jenny?" Dad pulls his white hanky out of his pocket and gives it to me.

"Should I call for an ambulance?" the desk lady says.

I blink a bunch of times. Try to sit up, but my arms are all rubbery, like Pokey and Gumby, and somebody's playing a big bass drum inside my head. "No ... no ... just dizzy," I manage to say. Then I lick the salty blood off my lips, check my teeth with my tongue. Did I knock one out?

Dad and Miss Dill each get an arm in underneath mine

and lift me up to my feet, like I'm a giant rag doll. Partway down the stairs, I hear her.

"Crumpled up like a busted balloon. You see her panties under that ugly hand-me-down dress? Those baby ones with the teddy bears on them?"

Their giggles sound like they're coming through the principal's P.A. system. Sarah even does some of her snort laughing. I look out from under my eyelashes in time to see the adjudicator stand up and shush them.

Where's Bugs Bunny and his magic paintbrush? I need a black hole to disappear me.

After the desk lady gets me a bag of ice, Dad helps me down the stairs and into the car.

"You'll be okay, sweetie. Just a bump on the old noggin and a fat lip. Nothing a few hours of television can't fix."

I groan. "Why'd that happen? What's wrong with me?"

He starts the car, then leans over and squeezes my shoulders. "Likely just a bad case of nerves. I used to feel sick to my stomach when I first started playing guitar in front of people. The lady working at the Festival said it happens a few times every year."

"Yeah, but it wasn't supposed to happen to me." It's hard to talk with my lips all swelled up like a split plum. "I'm a good singer. Better than dumb Sarah Saunders."

"Shhh … Just lean back and relax, Jenn. We'll be home in no time."

I yawn and close my eyes. Next thing I know, Old Red's crunching up the driveway, then Dad's helping me out of the car. Mom doesn't say anything when she sees him piggybacking me up the front walk. Just hands over Bethy, then wraps her arms around me. Helps me get settled under the rainbow afghan on the living room couch, then sits down beside me and pats my hand. Doesn't even ask any questions. Until the tears start coming, like Niagara Falls. Skippy trots over and starts licking my face.

Mom gets me some Kleenex, waits for the Falls to dry up. "Oh, Jenny. What can I do to make it better?"

I move the soggy ice sack and feel the bump with my fingertips. Gently. "Ouch!" I lick my fat lip. "What happened?"

She smiles. "You fainted. Don't you remember?"

I shake my head, then squinch my eyes closed again. The drummer's still banging away inside my head. But then I do remember. Sarah's face, with her big *Alice in Wonderland* cat's teeth grinning up at me.

"Must have been nerves. Or maybe you're coming down with something."

"I didn't know there'd be so many people there. W ... w ... watching." I snuff back some snot. "It's scary. And Sarah ... she laughed!"

"Oh, honey. It's over now. You'll have lots of other chances to sing."

I gulp a few times, then start sniffling again. "But I practiced so hard. I wanted to win. Show everybody how g-g-good I can sing. Like Annie Murray. How am I ever g-g-gonna be on *Singalong Jubilee* if I'm all the time fainting?"

"I'll give Miss Dill a call later to let her know you're all right," Mom says. "Dad said she was very worried about you."

"Can you ask her who won?" I try to blow my nose. But it hurts. "I know it wasn't Sarah. She sounded like a crow with laryngitis. Same as always."

"Let me help you up to your room," Mom says. "I don't think we need to worry about a concussion. Sounds to me like your brain's working just fine!"

Before Mom starts cooking supper, she brings Bethy in for a cuddle. "Want me to sing my song for you, Bethy?" She gives me a big grin, shows me her new bottom teeth. "It won't be that good, because of my puffy lip." When I'm done, I try to get her to clap hands, but she giggles and pulls my hair instead.

Dad comes into my room during the night a couple of times, shines a flashlight right into my eyeballs to check my pupils. The bright light kills my eyes, so guess they're working all right. "I can't stop thinking about it," I say. "I looked so stupid. And I wanted to win."

He turns off the flashlight. "*If at first you don't succeed, try, try again*," he says.

"Is that supposed to make me feel better? Because it doesn't. Not at all."

"I know you, Jenny. You're not the giving-up kind. Sleep tight."

After he leaves, I still can't get to sleep, so I get Bren's letter out of my orange crate nightstand. Add a P.S. right beside the smiling ladybug in the corner.

P. S. You can't believe what happened at the Music Festival. I fainted! It was almost as bad as the time I peed my pants when I was doing Show and Tell in Grade 1. Or the time I forgot to take off my flowery baby doll bottoms and Junior lifted up my skirt so the whole world could see. I hope Mom lets me stay home tomorrow.

The only good thing is Miss Creelman said we're getting a new girl. Even if it is almost the end of the year. I hope she'll be nice and that she'll want to be my friend.

How do you like Cape Breton Island? Did your mom say you can move back to Springhill yet?

Your BEST Friend

Jenn (Nature Club President)

CHAPTER 3

(WHEREIN The New Girl Arrives)

"I see London, I see France, I see Blinky's underpants!" Soon as I walk through the door in the morning, Sarah starts chanting, with Penny and Vickie hee-hawing around her, doing their jackass laughs, which is not a swear word but another word for donkey.

"You should've been there," Sarah says. "Her dress was all up around her belly. The whole world, boys and all, got a real good look at her teddy-bear panties and her undershirt!"

"I used to wear those ... in kindergarten," Vickie says.

Penny giggles. "At least she wasn't wearing one of her sister's diapers."

"No," Sarah says. "But I think she might have peed her pa ..."

"Shhh!" Miss Creelman claps her hands. "One, two, three! Eyes on me!"

I look up. Everybody looks up.

She never told us the new girl would be brown.

Mud-puddle brown.

Her too-big clothes hang off her, like a scarecrow left out all winter. She's got mad, skinny eyes, and her hair's shiny and blue-black, like coal. Goes almost to her bum.

I try to tuck my own bits of hair behind my ears. The bees in the back corner whisper and buzz.

"Good morning, boys and girls. Please join me in welcoming the newest member of our Springhill Memorial family." Miss Creelman's got the same smile as Jerome, the Friendly Giant's giraffe friend on TV. Chiclet teeth, big eyes, long curly lashes. She folds her hands together in front of her wide red belt. "Melody: Melody Summer Syliboy. Isn't that a deliciously melodious name? Makes me want to burst into song!"

Nobody says anything. Not out loud at least.

I'd sooner fall into a smelly coal pit than be a new girl in Grade 4 at Springhill Memorial. Especially a brown girl with a flakey name like Melody Syliboy.

Miss Creelman tells her to sit in the empty desk right next to mine. I give her my polite church smile, but Melody Summer Syliboy's busy, rolling her new pencil back and forth, back and forth, in its wooden groove. And humming. Only it's mad humming. Like she hates our guts already, before she even knows us.

When the recess bell goes, Miss Creelman stands up, then wiggles her finger for me and Melody to come to her desk.

"Jennifer, would you be a doll and show Melody around, then take her outside? She might like to meet some of the other teachers, and you know Miss Dill real well."

I blush and rub my bump. "Um ... Mom gave me this note so I could stay inside today and rest. My head's still aching. I think I have a concussion."

She takes the note and smiles down at Melody, then pats her arm. Melody jerks her shoulder away and steps back. Miss Creelman gives her a funny look. "Oh, um ... of course. I forgot." She sits down at her desk and picks up a long sheet of paper. "Melody, dear, you haven't filled in your father's name on the registration form."

"He's deceased," Melody mumbles.

Did she say diseased? Like measles or the mumps?

Miss Creelman puts one hand over her mouth. "Oh, I'm so sorry." She coughs and looks away. "Sarah, could you please show Melody around?"

Sarah rolls her eyes. "Really?"

Miss Creelman presses her orange lips together, crosses her arms in front of her belt.

"Oh, all right. Come on, then, Silly Boy."

"Her name's Melody," Vickie says. "Isn't it?"

The new girl keeps her eyes on the floor while the rest of them push past us through the doorway. Doesn't say anything, just shuffles behind Sarah out into the hallway. I'm cold, so I tiptoe out behind them and get my sweater off my coat hook.

All at once, the gigantic hall windows start rattling. When

the floor takes to vibrating, everybody hunkers down, waits for the bump to finish. Melody freezes and her brown eyes open wide, like Bambi's after the rifle shot. Nobody tells her that it's only the coal, reminding us it's still there, way down in the mine tunnels.

"I like your sweater," Sarah says to Melody when the bump's over. "Wade Skidmore's got the same one, only red and blue stripes instead of brown and black."

The new girl shoves her arms into the sleeves, then buttons her sweater right up under her chin. Stares down at her bunchy brown leotards and black shoes.

"You hear I almost won yesterday, Blinky?" Sarah says. "Well, I tied for fifth, at least. Got an 82." She stares at my bump. "You turning into one of your Nanny's billy goats?"

Wish I was *a billy goat so I could ram you with my horns. But since I'm a girl, I'd be a nanny goat.* I try to cover the lump with my bangs and go back into the classroom. I put on my soft blue sweater, the one Nanny made me that matches the tiny one she knit for Bethy. I sit down at my desk and get my book out of the drawer under my seat. Why can't I have a twin like the Bobbseys?

After recess, the Bad Boys slouch in late. Junior Tattrie and Wade Skidmore. Junior's yellow hair's going in fifty different directions, like he sucked on his finger then stuck it in a plug. His shirt's all tucked into his underwear that's pulled up way higher than his pants, like somebody gave him a wedgie—only nobody'd dare to. Wade's starting to get whiskers. He failed Grade Primary *and* Grade 1.

"Excuse me, boys." Miss Creelman turns around and looks at the clock. "Nice of you to join us, even at this late hour. Why, pray tell, were you detained?"

"Principal had us in the office," Wade mumbles. "Something about a broken window out back."

Junior grins, shows the whole world his green pond-scummy teeth. His lips pretty near stretch from one pig ear clear across to the other. Holds out his hands so everybody can see the red marks from the leather strap, then plops down in the desk on the other side of mine. "Hey, Jennifer. Wanna show us your underpants?"

Wade takes to laughing like somebody's tickling him.

Miss Creelman raps her pointer on Wade's desk, just missing his filthy fingers. Melody jumps, then claps her hands over her ears and shrinks down into her seat. "That's enough of that, boys. Open your math books to the long division problems on page 192."

When she goes back to the front of the class, Junior hisses over at me. "Did ya pee your pants again, too, Blinky? Psssssss …"

My ears get all hot. I open up my math scribbler and get to work. Keep one eye on the clock and wait for summer.

Friday morning, everybody's buzzing around the bulletin board when I get there. "You look so pretty, Sarah," Vickie says. "Like a model in the Eaton's catalogue."

"Yeah. That's the New York dress I was telling you about. Can you believe Blinky? Looks like she's trying to stuff her whole hand in her mouth!"

The newspaper reporter! At recess, I wait 'til everybody else goes outside, then I stroll over to the bulletin board, make like I'm looking out the window. I've always wanted to have my picture in the paper. Only I'm all hunched over in this one and my mouth's wide open, everything but my thumb stuffed into it. My bad eye's half shut and my cowlick's sproinging out like a horn. Beside me, Sarah looks like a perfect princess. Except she's really an evil Queen. Queen Smirkle Bee of the Hip Hive.

Dear Bren:

Sarah's getting meaner every day. I finally got my picture in the paper for the Music Festival but I look stupid in it. Chewing on my nails and looking nervous. Like a cat in a room full of rocking chairs is what Nanny would say.

We're having lots of little bumps here lately. Hope there isn't ever another BIG BUMP! The new girl doesn't seem that friendly. Her name's Melody.

I miss you,
Your BEST Friend,
Jenn

CHAPTER 4

(WHEREIN Nanny Smells a Thief)

I try to open my mouth to sing. But my lips are glued together and I'm suffocating. I hold my twitchy bad eye open and stare into the darkness—at the gawking eyes, dozens of yellow cat eyes, glowing in the dark. And underneath them, teeth, big white smirkle teeth. I clap my hands over my ears when the donkey laughs and whispery buzzing start echoing off the ...

I yank the covers down off my face, sit up, and take a big, slow breath. The sun's shining right in on me, and somebody's cooking bacon downstairs. I fall back on my pillow, close my eyes again, wait a few seconds for my heart to stop racing, then get up.

"Want to help me with Nanny's storm windows?" Dad asks, after we're done our pancakes. "Should've done it weeks ago."

"Hang on. I'm just reading Bren's letter again."

Dear Jenn:

I'm starting to forget what you look like. Did you grow since Easter? One person I don't miss is Sarah. I don't have any friends here yet. But one girl did ask me to her birthday party. I think her mother made her. We're going deep-sea fishing! Hope Karen's dad has life jackets so the Breath Grabber won't get me if I fall overboard!

Anyway, it's time for school. I miss you more than you miss me.

Your BEST Friend, Bren

I fold up the letter and stuff it back in its lilac envelope. "If we can take Sir Skips A Lot, since Bren's not here this year."

"Want to go for a ride, Good Knight?" Dad asks. "Get your leash!"

"*Woof!*" Skippy prances over to the front door and picks his leash off the hat rack with his teeth. Sits there sweeping his tail back and forth across the floor, dancing the dust bunnies into the corners. Not acting much like the handsome Knight in shining armor he used to be when Bren and me dressed him up.

I'm still getting used to the new prison on Herrett Road. It looks spooky as always, perched up there on top of the hill like some haunted castle. The prisoners are out in the fields, working with pickaxes and shovels. There's one standing real close to the fence. Looks like Elvis. And he's singing. I turn my head away when he catches me staring, nods and smiles at me. Dad's singing, too, a country song about Folsom Prison blues. I roll my window up and come in on the chorus, but I stop when I see somebody running through the cow pasture on the other side of the road.

"Hey, there's the new girl."

Melody's got a paper lunch sack in her hand. I twist around and stare out the back window as Dad slows down for the bobby pin turn after Wakeup Hill. She runs through the long dead grass, then walks up to the old split elm tree in the middle of the pasture. Looks all around, then drops the sack down inside it and runs back toward the road, waving. Is she waving at me? I look back over my other shoulder. The Elvis prisoner's waving, too. Or maybe he's just swatting flies.

"That's funny. Why would she be putting a lunch sack in that tree?"

"Maybe she collected some acorns for the chipmunks," Dad says.

"Mmm … maybe. Only why would she leave them in the bag?"

Soon as we turn off Black River Road onto Nanny's lane, I roll my window down all the way. Skippy puts his front paws on my legs, sticks his snout out, closes his eyes, and sniffs like he's trying to suck up the whole world. Until a rabbit runs out of the woods in front of us and Dad slams on the brakes. Then Skippy just about falls right out and starts howling like a wolf.

Nanny's hanging sheets on the line and watching for us on the back porch. She's not the hugging type; she's all business, is what Dad says. Like an army sergeant. Starts giving us orders before we even get the car doors shut.

"Don't track any dirt in. Just got done waxing the floors. Peculiar thing—I hung three old wool blankets out to air last night. Lo and behold, there was only two to pull in this morning. Holey as a lace doily, but I use 'em by the front door, rolled up to keep out the draft." She bends down and picks something up. "Even more peculiar, this dandy little twig basket was setting right here on the porch waiting for me when I got up. Perfect for my clothes pegs."

"Maybe the forest fairies got cold during the night. Like in *The Elves and the Shoemaker*. Only they left a basket instead of shoes," I say. "Wish I could make a basket like that."

"Humph." Nanny's got her jean overalls on, and her long kinky gray hair's all tied up in a tight ball of braids on the back of her head. She's got Granny Clampett glasses, but she's not as crazy as Granny, and, far as I know, she's never cooked possum. Or, if she did, she never told us. She does make rabbit stew, but Mom says I don't have to eat it.

"We had our first escape from the new prison two nights ago," Dad says. "Best keep your doors and windows locked at night, Ma."

"So long as your father's twenty-two's hanging right here

by the back door, I'll be just fine." She gives the long shotgun on the wall a nod as we follow her and her laundry basket inside the back porch. "Fine and dandy. Upon my soul, I can't hardly breathe in this old place, come spring. Oh, no you don't." Nanny drops her basket and slams the porch door fast, so Skippy bangs his black gumdrop nose on it and yelps. Then he stands up on his back legs and walks around like a furry person, whining and staring in the window at us. Nanny shakes her finger at him. "Knight or no knight, you're still a critter, and critters belong outside."

Dad and I look at each other and try not to laugh. If Nanny thinks Skippy's funny, she doesn't let on.

"Getting the windows open keeps me from going doolally, allows me to blow off some of the winter stink, keep my brain from addling." She hangs her blue cardigan on its peg beside the door and steps out of her clunky gardening shoes into her slippers.

I put my rubber boots next to her shoes on the mat.

"Sort of like letting your feet out to air after having wool socks on all day," Dad says.

"Ewww, Dad. Stinky feet—that's gross." I lick my lips and look at the full glass cookie jar on the counter. "Smells like cookies to me. Coconut oatmeals." I don't tell Nanny it smells like moth balls, too, the ones she uses to keep hungry moths from nibbling away at all her balls of yarn up in the attic.

"Help yourself—take me a month of Sundays to eat all those. I can't seem to stop baking even though your grampy—God rest his soul—and his giant sweet tooth are long gone." She looks up at the ceiling. "Hope the other Big Bump widows aren't still as lonesome as me."

"You're welcome to move into town with us anytime," Dad says. "You know that."

She stares over top her glasses at him. "Yes, Robert. And who do you expect would look after my animals and my garden then? Can't afford a hired hand."

Dad says he doesn't need my help with the windows, so Nanny takes me into her little sewing room off the kitchen. "I've got some stitching to do—why don't you help get my old photo albums in order? Trying to get them put to rights before God calls me to join his choir." She sits down at her sewing machine. "Maybe you could sing something for me, Jennifer Elizabeth. Some of the Lord's music."

I get the Pot of Gold chocolate box full of photographs off her needlepoint shelf, then open up the first big album, start turning the pages real slow. Every single picture's got the date scribbled onto it. Some of the pictures are slipping out of the little black triangle corners that hold them in place. Nanny gets real cross if they fall out. I re-lick some of the triangles, start tucking the pictures back into them, and sing.

"Jesus loves me, this I know, for the Bible tells me so ..." Nanny tries to sing along, but I think she forgets the tune.

"Dad didn't look much like Bethy when he was a baby," I say. "He's bald as the Man in the Moon."

"He had a little hair—between the ages of three and

twenty." Nanny says over the whirring of her sewing machine needle going up and down. "Same as his father."

"Where's this building?" I hold up the page so she can see. It's a brown and white picture of a dark old stone building with lots of windows, but even the windows look black. There's no trees or grass or anything around it, just dirt. "Is it a jail?"

She stops sewing and stares at me. "How'd you get that goose egg on your noggin?"

"I ... uh ... I fell at school." I try to cover it with my bangs. "What's this building?"

"Oh, that." She snorts. "The Indian school down in Shubenacadie."

"Did you go to school there?"

She glares at me. "I look like an Indian to you? Used to work there, umpteen years ago."

I shiver. "It looks spooky. Were you a teacher?"

"Last time I checked, teachers needed to have their Grade 12 diploma. I had to leave school and start farming with my daddy the year I turned twelve. Worked in housekeeping at the school in the early 1940s. Before we moved up here to Springhill."

"Did you like it?"

"Humph! The work was all right, but some of those kids sure did need to have the Indian trounced right out of them. They were all the time stealing stuff. Couldn't turn your back or they'd rob you blind, then poke fun at you for not being able to see."

"But you're not blind," I say.

She frowns at me. "That's just an expression. And the screaming and whooping that went on! Just like in the movies—talking some kind of mumbo jumbo I couldn't make hide nor hair of and sassing the Father and the Sisters. Don't even get me started on the fighting. Screeching like scrapping raccoons."

"Were they all bad? At my school there's only a few bad kids."

She stops the machine and stares out the window at the tire swing in the willow tree. "There was one girl. Pretty little thing. Now, what was her name ... Patricia. Peppermint Patty I called her. Kept peppermints in my pocket for her. Pink was her favorite." Nanny smiles. "Used to help me peel the vegetables. Called me Mrs. Parsnips."

"She must've liked you."

She nods, then goes back to scowling. "Most times the lazy parents didn't even visit the kids. Probably busy dipping into the hooch and thankful somebody else was taking care of their little devils, showing them how to behave off the reservation. Teaching them to be Christian. Wouldn't trust an Indian far as I could throw him."

"They lived at that school?" I say. "They even slept there?"

"Yup. Likely the cleanest beds they ever saw, except that they were all the time wetting them, making more work for yours truly. Something wrong with their waterworks," she says. "Don't know where they'll end up now they're closing the Residential School. Far from here, is all I hope."

"I'm glad I'm not an Indian," I say. "My school's not that bad. But some of the kids are mean like that. Only I can understand what they're saying, even when I wish I didn't."

When Dad's done taking off the storm windows, Nanny and me go around moving her purple African violets off the windowsills and sliding up all the heavy windows. It's only drizzling a little by then, and the breeze makes the flowery curtains flap around inside.

I follow Nanny to the front hall. She leans out the tall, skinny window beside the stairs, closes her eyes, and sucks in some air. "Upon my soul, I can smell summer on that south wind, can't you, Jennifer?"

I stick my head out and take a deep breath, but all I can smell is the cookies and the mothballs. I nod anyway. "Smells like worms," I say. "And melting poopsicles." I giggle when my stomach growls. "Wish summer would get here so I didn't have to go to school."

"Tsk! Tsk! *All good things come to she who waits*," Nanny says. "Mercy, Jennifer, you're impatient as a hungry bossy bellowing for mama's milk."

"Why do you call cows bossy again?" I ask. "I forget."

She smiles and her face crinkles up like an apple doll. "Didn't you ever hear Daisy mooing? She's nothing if she's not bossy!"

"Oh, yeah."

"Now my stomach's grumbling. I've got a hankering for some fried Spam and potato hash." She takes her checkered apron off its hook and ties it around her waist. "You can peel the spuds, then fetch a jar of bread and butter pickles from the cold room."

When everything's ready, I ring the cowbell on the back porch. A few minutes later, Dad comes banging and stomping in from the barn. He's wearing an old plaid barn jacket that's a little too small for him. We sit down at the kitchen table. Dad sits in Grampy's old spot, like always.

"Daisy looks almost ready to calve," he says. "She's got that birthing glow about her."

Nanny nods and hitches up her overalls. "Any day now. Shouldn't be a problem for that bossy; this'll be her fifth baby."

"Can we come see the calf soon as it's born?" I ask. "Remember when Rosie was born—her wobbly stick legs?"

Nanny puts one crooked finger in front of her lips to shush me. "Don't talk with your mouth full, Jennifer Elizabeth."

I finish chewing, then swallow. "Sorry, Nanny."

"I'll give you a call. Could be I'll need a hand cleaning up and picking out a name. You did a good job picking Buttercup. Suits that barn cat to a T."

"How about Sarah? She's this girl I know that's real bossy."

"I'm partial to flower names myself," Nanny says. "Pansy, or Lily. Maybe Violet."

"What if it's a boy?"

"Hmmm ... I'd have to sit and ponder on that for a while," she says.

"What about Daffy, like daffydill? Daffy Duck's a boy."

"Possible." Then she frowns over her glasses at me. "But not probable."

When we're done eating, Nanny runs the hot water in her big old-fashioned white sink. The same sink Dad used to take bubble baths in when he was little.

"Want to take a walk out to the coal cave?" Dad asks me.

I look at the pile of dirty dishes, then back at Nanny.

She shakes her head and waves me away. "No, you two go on. Take that foolish prancing Knight with you. And don't forget to put your father's old jacket back in the barn after. Keeps me company when I'm doing my chores."

The woods smell fresh and clean, like Dad's Old Spice shaving lotion. Some late Mayflowers are peeking their tiny pink bud faces out from under the dead leaves. Over top of last year's tall grass rustling, we hear a spooky warbling sound. Like a bird's being murdered.

I grab onto Dad's hand. "What's that?"

"Sounds to me like there's loons on Sandy Bottom Lake this year. Haven't heard them for years. That's their warning cry—must think we sound dangerous. Like foxes maybe. I expect they've got a young one or eggs to protect."

"Maybe we can go see them in the summer." I start to skip, which is not that easy in my big boots. "Lost my partner, what'll I do? Lost my partner, what'll I do? Skip to my loo, my darlin.'"

I freeze when I see something move out of the corner of one eye. "What's that?"

Skippy barks and starts doing his prancing.

When Dad follows my finger, there's nothing there. Only trees and bushes. "Just your imagination," he says. "Nobody ever comes out here. Not since your grampy passed."

"Did Grampy really dig coal out of the cave? To burn in the furnace?"

Dad nods. "There's coal tunnels everywhere under the ground in these parts. Not too often they make themselves known. That sinkhole just appeared here one day—1955, I believe it was. Nobody knows exactly what causes the bumps that make the ground cave in, but Grampy sure did appreciate the free heat."

"Don't bears live in caves?" I ask.

"Now that you mention it, the sinkhole would make a nice bear's den."

My eyes bug open.

"Kidding," he says. "Never seen any sign of bears in these woods." He puts his arms around me and Skippy. "Just the hugging kind."

"Hey, somebody moved the branches away," I say when we get to the coal cave. "Maybe there *is* somebody down there." I look up in the direction of the prison and whisper. "Maybe that escaped prisoner."

Skippy puts his nose to the ground, like it's a magnifying glass. Paws at the dead grass and snorts, like a pig looking for grubs.

Dad shakes his head and laughs. "As good a hiding place as that would be, don't think anybody'd want to crawl down into that black hole. Except possibly a critter."

"Maybe a fox. Or skunks."

"That sinkhole's an accident waiting to happen. Filling it back in with dirt would be the best idea, but that would be one doozey of a pile of dirt."

I get down on my hands and knees on top of one of the pine branches and try to see into the cave. Skippy drops down on his belly next to me. "It's real dark in there. And deep. It'd be the best hiding place for Hide and Seek—only I'd never be brave enough. How did Grampy get down inside such a deep hole?"

Dad crouches down beside me. "Deep is right. Too deep for a regular ladder. We tied that rope to the big maple over there, lowered ourselves down into the hole, just to see how deep it was. More than twenty feet. About as tall as Nanny's house. But when we got down there, guess what we found?"

"Ghosts? Skeletons?"

Dad laughs. "Nope. A giant spruce tree."

"Trees can grow inside caves?"

He shakes his head. "Must've blown down in a storm, or maybe a bump, and fallen into the hole. Now, your grampy was a real smart man—not book-smart, but he was a thinker. He took a good hard look at that tree lying there, walked around it, pacing it off. "More than thirty feet" he told me. Then he did a peculiar thing. He started singing. *We are climbing Jacob's Ladder* ... Made quite an echo down there."

"I know that one. From Sunday school. It's the ladder angels use to get to Heaven."

Dad nods. "Anyway, we chopped most of the branches off one side of that big old spruce. Spun it around so it was pointing to the opening, then Grampy told me to get in ahead of him, in under the skinny part of the trunk. We took baby steps toward the thick part and pushed up at the same time. Then we inched the tree back toward the opening. Step, push, pull. Step, push, pull. Took a while, and a lot of grunting if I remember correctly, but we finally got the top ten feet or so up over the edge of the hole."

"Then you climbed up like monkeys?"

"You bet—Grampy got lots of exercise going up and down his Jacob's Ladder. Used the rope to haul up the buckets of coal."

"That would be a fun ladder." I look all around the edge of the hole. "Is it still there?"

Dad shook his head. "That was more than a dozen years ago. Expect the tree's all rotted away by now. Don't know how safe the rope would be anymore, either."

We drag the branches over across the tunnel opening and turn back toward Nanny's house. I keep hold of Dad's hand the whole entire way.

Dear Bren:
I had to write to you again already because there's an escaped prisoner running loose! Nanny had a blanket stolen right off her clothesline. But whoever took it left her a cute little stick

basket so I don't think it's a mean criminal. The police are even offering a reward—$200!

Nanny has a picture of an old school that looks like a jail. She called it the Indian school. Said she used to work there and that the kids were all bad. I feel sorry for them, having to live at an ugly school like that and never getting to go home. Remember when we used to want to be Indians? Riding horses bareback and living in teepees. But some of the ones in the movies and on TV are scary. Like the Bad Boys.

I hope your new school is nice and that there aren't any Bad Boys there.

I miss you ...

Jenn

CHAPTER 5

(WHEREIN The Queen Smirkle Bee Does Not Like Indians)

Just before the start of summer, Dad and me take Skippy down to the ball field beside the school after supper one night to play fetch. Sarah, Penny, and Vickie are sitting in one of the building's big stone window frames. "The Hip Hive," they call it. Bren and me used to sit in one of the windows at the back of the school to have our Nature Club meetings. Wonder if Bren took her pumpkinseed snowflakes to Cape Breton with her.

"Hello, Mr. Parsons," Sarah calls out. "Isn't it a lovely evening? Hi, Jennifer. Want to play with us?" Says it like I'm her best friend. "You can use my skipping rope."

I shake my head. "Don't have time."

"Oh," she says. "Do you have to get home to practice your

singing?" When Dad looks away and goes to throw the ball for Skippy, she jiggles her legs, waves her arms around, makes like she's about to faint.

"Here, Skippy. Fetch!" Dad yells.

When Skippy brings the baseball back to me, I throw it hard. As far away from the girls as I can. Dad whistles and claps. "Nice arm, Jenn." Skippy takes off after it like he's chasing the neighbor's cat. I'm right behind him.

Next time I throw it, the ball goes into the wild rose bushes in the empty lot behind the ball field. While Dad goes whistling off to root around in the thorny branches, I sit down next to Skippy, lean my head up against his, and scratch his floppy ears. Act like I'm not watching Sarah, only I am.

She's got one of her tall white boots stuck out in front of her. Boots made for walking, like in Nancy Sinatra's song. I try to pay attention to Skippy, only Sarah's spitting out her words so they blast out over the whole entire playground.

"Guess what My Mother said." She stands up, bounces up and down on her shiny white toes. Doesn't bother waiting for them to guess. "We-e-e-e-l-l-l ... she was working at the church rummage sale, on Saturday? And you know that ugly jumper I had last year? The green corduroy one? The new girl's mother wanted to buy it. And ..."

When she stops to take a breath, my bad eye takes to twitching. I start singing inside my head, thinking about her white boots walking all over everybody.

"... get this—she didn't even have *twenty-five cents* to pay for the jumper!" Sarah does some of her snort laughing.

"Is that true?" Penny asks.

Sarah spins around and looks down at her. "My Mother knows *everything*!"

Ha! Liar, liar, pants on fire. Her Royal Lowness doesn't seem to know much about being nice and neighborly.

I don't want to keep listening, but it's like driving by a dead critter on the road—I try not to look, only I can't help it.

And then I see the new girl.

All hunkered down, up against the fence, behind the biggest horse chestnut tree.

Like a cornered mouse.

Sarah aims her sharp chin at Melody. Shakes out her skipping rope, squeezes the handles, and gets this fake smile on. The Queen Smirkle Bee of the Hip Hive. Makes like she's gonna give her buzzing bees a real nice present.

"And My Mother ..." She starts skipping. "... says I am *never* to play with her because ..." The rope slaps the hard dirt, faster and faster, until she's doing pepper. "... *they're* not like *us* ..." Slap. Slap. Slap. "They're dirty wild *Indians*!"

I start coughing like I just swallowed a giant gumball. The girls all point their eyes over at the new girl. Sarah's grinning her crazy *Alice in Wonderland* cat grin.

I press my cheek up against Skippy's soft head, and blink so my eyes'll stop watering.

When I open them again, Melody's right beside me. "You okay? You need a drink?"

I look up at her. She doesn't look much like the Lone Ranger's friend, Tonto, or the Indians fighting with the cowboys on TV Westerns. Except for her black hair and brown skin. And she's a whole lot quieter. Unless she's pretending.

"Well, isn't that sweet? Blinky and Silly Boy," Sarah says. "A perfect pair of hand-me-down ragamuffins."

I stop coughing and shake my head. When Melody reaches out to pat Skippy, I take hold of his collar and walk away, fast, toward Dad's bald head that's sticking up out of the rose bushes.

I'm still thinking about grabbing Sarah's skipping rope and wrapping it around her chicken neck, when the earth starts shaking and grumbling under my feet. Like somebody's using a jackhammer. Only lasts for a couple of seconds. "Just a little bump," Dad says, pulling his arm up out of the thorny branches. "Ta da! The coal reminding us it's still there." He tosses me the ball and clips Skippy's leash onto his collar. "Let's go home, partners."

I look back over my shoulder, but the playground's empty. Wonder if anybody warned the new girl yet about the bumps and the sinkholes.

Dear Bren:

Today I found out that the new girl is an INDIAN. Like on the Lone Ranger. Sarah and Her Royal Lowness don't like Indians, same as Nanny. This is going to be a very long summer. I wish Bethy was bigger so she could play with me. I went to visit Nanny's new calf Daffy yesterday. But it wasn't much fun without you. I have to take swimming lessons again and I'm going to read lots of books and work hard on my singing. I really want to sing a solo in Grade 5. But I need to learn not to faint. I want to learn to sing the cool part too. So far in choir I always sing the regular part. The melody. I forget the name of the other part, but I want to learn it.

I hope you did not find a new best friend yet. But I do hope you have a friend (or two).

Your BEST Friend,

Jenn

CHAPTER 6

(WHEREIN The Milk Goes Missing)

I get up before the sun the first morning of swimming lessons. I'm scared to get water up my nose and in my ears, but I can almost do ten bobs in a row in the bathtub now without drowning. And I can swim, only not without a flutter board or a life jacket. It's my third summer taking lessons. If I don't pass this year, Bethy might get a badge before me!

I find Bren's last letter in my orange crate and read it again.

Dear Jenn:
I don't have to take swimming lessons this year because Karen's family has their very own

swimming pool! And we swim there almost every day. We're going to overnight summer camp the same week too.

You're a real good singer—remember when you tried to teach me the words to Puff the Magic Dragon? I still remember some of them. And how Bethy made that little pigeon sound when you sang it to her. Is she big now?

It rains a lot in Cape Breton but I don't think there are any Indians here. Does the new girl wear her hair in braids like on TV? I don't have time to write much—Karen just called and it's pool time! After that she's going to teach me how to make an origami owl.

Your Friend, Bren

What's an origami owl? I put the letter away, then push my window up and stick my head out, look for a wishing star in the pink and gray morning sky. *Star light, star bright, last star I see tonight.* Last star works just as good as first star. *Please let Bren come visit me in the summer. Without Karen.* When Skippy woofs from down in the back porch, I look over by the garbage cans, but there's no raccoons rattling the lids. I'm just about to pull my head back in when something moves. Some*body* moves. In the back field, just behind the red metal swing set over by the shed. Somebody with long hair—only it's running like a boy. I blink a couple of times but, when I look again, there's nobody there.

I pull my head back in and slam the window shut. Pull down my blind and crawl back into bed. Shiver, chew on my nails, and wait for the sun to come up.

When I hear Dad's electric razor buzzing in the bathroom, I get up and look out my window again. The clouds look like somebody painted them with a brush: white with pink edges. No hippie strangers running through the back pasture, though. Maybe I was still half asleep and dreaming.

"It's the strangest thing," Mom says when I get downstairs. "I put two empty milk bottles with two tokens out last night, and when I went to bring the milk in this morning, both empties and tokens were gone, but there was only one full bottle there. And these." She holds up a bunch of pink and white lilacs.

I take a big sniff. "Mmmm ... you sure you put out two?" Should I tell her what I saw?

"Positive. We're almost completely out, and Bethy's drinking practically a whole quart herself these days."

"Maybe the milkman made a mistake. I'll have cinnamon toast instead of Fluffs." I get the cinnamon sugar bowl out of the cupboard while she fills a vase with water for the flowers. "Thought I saw somebody in the backyard. Before the sun came up."

She turns to look at me. "That early? Who was it?"

I shrug. "Maybe I was sleepwalking. Didn't recognize them, anyway."

"We better make sure the doors are locked," she says. "And keep your blinds closed at night."

"You walking with me to swimming lessons?" I ask, between buttery bites of cinnamon toast.

"Bethy'd probably like to get out for a stroll since it's such a nice day. Maybe we'll take a picnic lunch. The laundry can wait."

When we get to the pool, there's only a few little kids and their mothers waiting outside the change room. I've already got my swimsuit on underneath my T-shirt and shorts so I don't have to get naked. I stuff my clothes and my sandals into an unlocked wire basket, put on my old green flip flops, and limp out onto the pool deck. I've already got flip flop blisters between my toes. Mom and Bethy are sitting outside the fence on the grass under a big maple tree.

The teacher's new. And bouncy. "Good morning, boys and girls," she shouts. "My name is Kathy. Kathy with a K." After we tell her our names, she claps her hands and says, "Everybody ready to work on their swimming this summer?" Hope she's not going to be one of those teachers that makes you jump right in the deep end the first day.

She is. "Okay. Now, most of you have taken swimming lessons before, so we're going to start by taking a dip in the deep end. I'm a firm believer in the power of plunging." She goes to the fence and gets down a long pole that's laying across two big hooks, walks back over to the edge with it. "I'll be standing right beside this sign for the twelve-foot end, holding onto this yellow pole. After you jump in, just open your eyes enough to see my pole, then work your way up it. Like a shinny pole on the playground. Easy as falling off a log, right, Jennifer?"

She says that to me since I'm the tallest kid in the class. Everybody else is about seven years old. Maybe six.

At least she's using the pole. My last year's teacher told us to jump in, then find our way back up to the sun. Which is not that easy on a cloudy day, with a three-thousand-pound water monster trying to drown you. "The Breath Grabber" is what Bren and me call it.

"Okay, Jennifer—why don't you go first? Show these little guys how it's done?"

I try to smile but it comes out wobbly, like my legs. I dig my last year's bathing suit out of my bum and walk toward her. My eye starts acting up, so I blink a bunch of times and rub it. Sing the scales up and down inside my head to distract myself. *C ... D ... E ... F ... G ... A ... B ... C.* She sticks the tall pole down in the water close to the high-diving board. *C ... B ... A ... G ... F ... E ... D ... C.* It completely disappears except for a few inches at the top.

"No snappy sharks!" Kathy with a K says. "Or angry alligators. Ready, Freddy?"

I look at her. Do I look ready? Do I look like a Freddy? Then I look down past my toes at the water. Can't see anything except for the ripply blue sky and a few clouds. My bad eye slams shut. I close the other one, take a deep breath, put on my rubber nose plug, squeeze it tight with my fingers. And jump.

Feels like a fire hose blasting half the pool straight into my ears. Right through to my brain. I kick my feet around, wiggle my toes, try to touch bottom so I can push myself back up. Only there's nothing but water, freezing cold water. I squint open my good eye and look all around for the yellow pole. It's gone! Did she forget about me?

I let go of my nose plug, pump both arms up and down, kick my feet as hard as I can, but the water's real heavy. And the Breath Grabber's got me. Squeezing hard, sucking all the breath right out of me. I spin around in circles, doing the eggbeater, opening and closing my fists, trying to find the pole. I'm running out of air fast. What's that? Cement— rough cement. I feel my way along the wall with my hands and feet, like a spider, trying to find the black twelve-foot sign painted on the wall. There it is! And the pole's right beside it. I grab onto it with both hands and feet and climb up it, like a monkey.

My head bursts out of the water just before my lungs burst inside of me. I'm too weak to pull myself up over the edge, so I hang there, coughing and barking like a seal, staring at the teacher's tanned feet. Kathy with a κ takes pity on me, leans over and gives me her hands. I scrape one knee, but I finally crawl out onto the deck and collapse on my belly. I lift my head and, out of my good eye, I see Mom's fingers grabbing onto the crisscross fence. She looks mad.

"See, boys and girls?" Kathy says. "Nothing to it! Now, who's next?"

I push myself up onto my knees and sit down on my bum.

Try to smile at the little kids, but I'm too busy gulping down mouthfuls of air like it's root beer.

I look around the deck for my towel. My eyes sting from the chlorine. And then I see them. Bright red painted toenails walking right up to my scratched leg. "What's wrong, Blinky? You look like you're half-dead."

"Yeah. You were in my class summer before last," Vickie says. "Weren't you?"

"Isn't this your third time in pre-beginners?" Sarah gives me her smirkle, then bugs her eyes open. "Nice nose-plug."

I yank off my nose-plug, leave it dangling around my neck, then turn around, hug my knees, and watch the next little kid jump in. Hope he finds the pole before the Breath Grabber finds him.

When the lesson's finally over, I change my clothes and go look for Mom and Bethy. They're sitting at a picnic table with Her Royal Lowness. She's talking loud enough for the whole park to hear her Queen voice. Only I don't think she ever lived in England.

"I had the same thing happen a couple of days ago," Mrs. Saunders says. "I needed three quarts of milk, but the milkman only left two."

"Maybe our regular man's on holidays," Mom says.

"No, I called the dairy and they checked with the driver. He's sure he left three."

"Maybe one of your neighbors borrowed one, then forgot about it," Mom says.

Mrs. Saunders shakes her head. "I asked everybody."

Then she leans in closer to Mom. "To be perfectly honest, Margie, I have my suspicions. There's a new family in town. Indians. And you know how *they* are. The girl's in Sarah's swimming class. I told Sarah to be sure and lock up the basket with her new summer clothes in it."

Mom zips her lips together. Gets that look on her face that means trouble. "No, Eva. I don't know how *they* are. In fact, I have not yet had the pleasure of meeting any Micmac people."

"Oh, yes." Mrs. Saunders waves her hand around in the air like she's swatting mosquitoes, then opens her purse and gets out a little mirror and her lipstick. Starts smearing some on. "My mother lives in Truro and had one in to do her spring cleaning last year. Brought more dirt into the house than she ever thought of cleaning out." She lights a cigarette and blows smoke out her nose. "And, I might add, some of Mother's heirlooms went missing at the same time. Several pieces of the family silver and a gold brooch."

Mom doesn't say anything after that. Turns to me instead. "How was your lesson, Jenny?"

I shrug. "Okay."

"Please excuse us. We're going to have our lunch now, Eva." Mom stands up and starts pushing the stroller with our red plaid picnic bag in it over to a different table. Her knuckles are white on the handle.

I carry Bethy over to the playground for a swing. Her Royal Lowness's voice follows us. "The girl will be in Jennifer and Sarah's class again in the fall. I can't imagine why they're closing the Indian school. Keep them on the reservations where they belong, I say."

"From what I understand," Mom says, "the Residential School was not the best place for any child to live. After all, what little girl or boy wants to live away from their parents in their formative years?" Her face is all pink and her blue eyes are flashing.

We get settled on the swing seat, and I'm just starting to make us go by pushing my toes off the dirt, when the ground starts trembling. I stop the swing and hold on tight to Bethy, pat her red curls. "It's okay, Bethy. Just the coal reminding us it's there." She giggles and grabs onto my nose. When the bump's done, we go back to sit at the picnic table with Mom. Mrs. Saunders is standing by the pool, with her pointy nose pressed up against the fence. "Try harder, darling. You can do better than that, Sarah."

Sarah climbs out of the pool, fiddles with the straps on her red Speedo, glares over at me. Tries to get me in her eye-lock, but I hold Bethy up in front of me and bury my face in her belly to hide my grin. "Whe-e-e-ere's Bethy? PEEK-a-boo!" I stop playing and put Bethy back down on my hip after Sarah turns away.

The person still in the water's swimming like I wish I could. She touches the wall on the other side, then does a somersault, like an otter, and swims back toward me. Climbs out of the pool, takes her bathing cap off, shakes her hair loose, and gives me a little smile.

"Nice job, Melody!" Kathy with a K says. "Are you sure

you've never taken swimming lessons before? Sarah, you need to work harder on your flutter kick. Put some effort into it."

I smile back at Melody and walk away.

Dear Bren:

I'm taking swimming lessons at the town pool—AGAIN. The teacher seems pretty nice, Kathy with a K. At least the Breath Grabber didn't drown me today. Melody's a real good swimmer, better than Sarah. Somebody's stealing milk around town. The funny thing is the thief left us some flowers. Almost like he was paying for the milk. It's a mystery!

I'm getting bored. When are you coming to visit? I'm so bored I'm reading all my old books again. Remember when your mom read Heidi out loud to us? I'm going to the library tomorrow. I'm going to see if they have A Girl of the Limberlost. It was Mom's favorite when she was little.

Your Not Drowned (yet!) Friend,

Jenn

CHAPTER 7

(WHEREIN Jenn Meets Elnora Comstock)

In the morning, I ride my banana bike—which is not really a banana bike, but my old blue bike with a purple banana seat and high handlebars stuck on—down to the library.

I got my own library card for my fifth birthday. The library lady, Mrs. Davidson, has a gray mustache and a whiskery mouse-nose mole on one eyebrow, but she was real nice about it when I forgot one of the "N's" in my name. Ripped up the first yellow card and gave me a brand new one. She never forgot my name after that, anyway.

"Good morning, Jennifer," she says. "You're up with our feathered friends this fine morning!"

"I'm bored." I slide my books in through the return slot. "Need some new books."

"Well, you've come to the right place. Somebody donated several titles for little girls just last week. They're in the children's section at the back. Shall I help you find something? I think there was a new Trixie Belden ..."

I shake my head. "That's okay." I close my eyes, walk between the shelves, run my fingers along the books, and breathe in the library smells—paper, musty old books, shiny new ones, and dust. *Mmmmm* ... I choose *The Pokey Little Puppy* to take home for Bethy. When I get to the Teen Fiction aisle, I tilt my head sideways and start looking at titles. Who did Mom say wrote that book? Somebody named Porter. Parker, Peterson ... here it is. Gene Stratton Porter—is that a boy or a girl? I take the heavy blue book off the shelf and flip through it to the last page. Four hundred and seventy-nine pages. I've never read a book that long before. I go back to the first page. And only four pictures in the whole thing! I sit cross-legged on the wooden floor in a patch of sunlight, turn to the first page, and start reading.

The front door opens and closes a few times, and I hear Mrs. Davidson talking to somebody, but I don't look up. The girl in the book's called Elnora Comstock. She's like me, with old clothes and messy hair, only her mom's always grouchy and her dad drowned. In the Limberlost swamp. She likes nature: trees, moths, and dragonflies. And she's not scared of anything—same as Bren.

When my eyelids start getting droopy, I stand up and stretch. Walk around to wake up my pins-and-needles feet.

I wander up the steps onto the little platform at the back of the library. Walk to the center and look out at all the books sitting politely on the shelves.

What if all the characters were alive?

Sitting there being bored, watching me, waiting for me to entertain them?

Nancy Drew, the Bobbsey twins, Heidi and her grandfather, Alice, the Hardy Boys. I look over at the desk. Mrs. Davidson's nowhere in sight, so I set my books down on the floor, fold my hands in front of me, and start singing, whisper-singing.

"Puff the magic dragon, lived by the sea ..." Instead of shelves of books, I see faces, friendly smiling, familiar faces. I sing a little louder and smile back at my audience. "... and frolicked in the autumn mist in a land called Honah Lee ..."

And then I see a real face.

A maple taffy face with long black hair.

The new girl.

I shut my mouth, pick up my books, and run back down the stairs. Straight to the desk.

"You found something, did you, dear?" Mrs. Davidson says. "Why is your face so red?"

I fan my face with the pages in the book. "It's hot in here," I say. "And ... um ... I'm in a hurry. I've got swimming lessons."

"Isn't this a little old for you, Jennifer?"

"Oh, no. I read books like this all the time. My mom's books."

"I read that one," a quiet voice behind me says. "It's real good."

I look back over my shoulder. "You did? I mean ... you can read English books?"

Melody looks confused but she smiles. "It was my mother's favorite."

I can't help myself. I turn right around and grin. "My mom's, too!"

"Having a common interest in books is often a good foundation for friendship." Mrs. Davidson stamps the red return date on my books and passes them back to me. "You know, it's the oddest thing, but when I came to work yesterday, I could tell someone had been digging in the outside return box. When I called a patron to remind him *Robinson Crusoe* was overdue, he said he'd left it in that box. I've never had books disappear from there before." She bends down and reaches underneath the counter. "But this was inside the return box. Isn't it lovely?" She holds up a picture. It's a pencil drawing of two chipmunks on a tree branch. The big one's reading a story to the little one.

"It looks like a camera picture," I say. "Whoever did it's a real good drawer. We had some milk go missing, too. And my Nanny had a blanket stolen off her clothesline. But the person left us presents, too—a twig basket and some lilacs." I remember what Her Royal Lowness said about Melody's family and look over at her. She's busy twisting her hair around her pointer finger and staring at the book in her hand. A fat one called *Gone With the Wind*.

The door squeaks open. Sarah and the Bad Boys. What are they doing at the library?

"I need to use the bathroom," Junior says.

"If you are asking my permission, then you must ask properly." Mrs. Davidson stabs her pencil into her bun.

"I did."

"No, you did not." Mrs. Davidson rests her elbows on the counter and folds her hands together. "The proper way is to say, 'Mrs. Davidson, may I *please* use the washroom?'"

He fiddles around with his fly and repeats what she said. Glares at me and pushes past us to the bathroom.

Wade looks at Melody. Stands real straight, like Tonto, puts one hand up in the air and says, "How."

Melody looks at her sneakers and hums. Quietly.

"Whatcha reading, Blinky?" Sarah tries to grab my fat book. "*A Girl of the Limberlost*—what kind of boring old book is that? Looks like a Bible. I'm reading my mother's Harlequin romances. Now, they're real interesting!"

I hold on tight to my books, say thank you to Mrs. Davidson, and walk toward the door.

"What're you doing in the library, Silly Boy?" I don't need to look back to tell that Sarah's giving Melody her smirkle. "Can you even read English? Or just mumbo-jumbo?"

"It's Melody," she answers.

"*What* did you say?"

I have to look back. Sarah's got a big purple vein bulging out of her forehead. Like she's got a garter snake squirming around in there.

"My name is Melody." Then Melody turns away and follows me out the door, stands on the steps, and watches me get on my bike.

Dear Bren:

Swimming lessons weren't so bad today. At least we stayed out of the Breath Grabber end. I'm reading a new book, A Girl of the Limberlost, about Elnora Comstock. Maybe you can find it at the Cape Breton library. Elnora's older than us but she could have been in our Nature Club. She catches moths and dragonflies and gets paid for them! She dresses funny and the other kids make fun of her. But she's really smart and nice. Sarah was being mean to Melody at the library today. She likes to read, too—like you and me. Melody I mean, not The Queen Smirkle Bee.

When are you coming to visit? Summer's almost over.

Your Best Friend, Jenn

CHAPTER 8

(WHEREIN Jennifer Starts Grade 5

and Plays MSG)

By the time school starts again, I'm on my third time reading *A Girl of the Limberlost*. But I'm skipping the boring parts this time. I didn't get a letter from Bren since she went to camp in July, so I don't know if she ever read it. Maybe I'll talk to Melody about the book. Mostly I like the parts when Elnora's in the swamp, but the mushy love parts are good, too.

Miss Creelman's our teacher again in Grade 5. I never had the same teacher two times before, but at least she's not new, like last year. And she lets us chew bubblegum on Friday afternoons, so long as we don't store it under our desks from one Friday to the next. Junior and Wade are the only ones gross enough to do that, anyway. Nanny says if you swallow gum, it stays in your stomach forever and plugs you up so you can't use the toilet. I put mine in the garbage, just in case she's right.

Tuesdays, we've got gym right after recess. After we get changed into our baggy blue gym rompers, the new gym teacher, Mr. MacLeod, takes us outside. Gives us free time since it's a nice sunny day. "Why don't you think up a game for the ladies to play, Sarah?" he says. "Something you can all enjoy together. We men are going to play a few innings of baseball."

I can throw a baseball farther than anybody, except for Wade. My old babysitter, Annie, showed me how, but the teacher doesn't ask if any girls want to play.

Sarah gives Melody her evil rat eye, then bats her eyelashes at Mr. MacLeod, like Ellie May Clampett. "Sure, Mr. MacLeod. I've got just the game."

We all make a circle around her. She stands in the middle with her hands on her hips. "Okay. It's a tag game I made up this summer," she says. "Me and Penny and Vickie."

"We did?"

Sarah gives Vickie a smirkle, then points her eyes sideways over at Melody. "Yeah, Chubby. You know ..."

Vickie and Penny giggle.

"It's called MSG. This is how it goes. I'll be IT first. When you tag somebody, you have to yell out 'MSG!' Then they've got the ger ... I mean, then they're IT."

Nobody says anything. "On the count of ten," she shouts. "One ... two ... three ..." I take off. I'm a fast runner and tag's my favorite gym game. When Sarah tags Vickie, sounds like she's yelling something about germs. I thought she said we were supposed to yell "MSG." Vickie tags Penny, only she screams out the new girl's name. I look around for Melody, but I don't see her anywhere.

I run along the fence and keep one eye on Penny. One of my sneakers comes untied and flies off; I stuff my foot back in, bend down to tie it fast.

Too late. Penny tags me, hard. "MSG!" she screams in my face. I can practically see her tonsils.

I take off after April. She's a slowpoke. "You're IT!" I poke her on the back. "MSG!"

By the time Mr. MacLeod blows his whistle, I'm laughing and shouting and running so hard that I almost forget to wonder what MSG stands for.

Until I see her.

MS. Playing tic-tac-toe in the dirt under the horse chestnut tree.

By her Germy self.

Does she know what MSG means?

I follow everybody to the gym door. "Can you believe all those dumb girls?" Sarah says. "I got them to play Melody Silly Boy Germs, and they didn't even know it. Even Mr. MacLeod didn't catch on. Isn't he dreamy?"

"He looks like the guitar player in the Monkees," Penny says.

"Silly Boy better not give me any real Indian germs," Sarah says. "Stinky germs."

"She couldn't really do that," Vickie says. "Could she?"

Melody keeps her eyes glued to her desk for the rest of the day, and she's all hunchy. Like the wheelchair people we sing Christmas carols for over at the Twin Elms. When Miss Creelman tells us to find a reading partner, Sarah grabs me.

"Be my partner, Jenn? You're the best reader, and runner."

I want to say no way, but instead I nod and giggle. Like Bethy when Dad tickles her belly with his bristly whiskers.

"Yes!" Miss Creelman says. "You can help Sarah get caught up on her reading, Jennifer."

I open up *The Bobbsey Twins Forest Adventure*, then wait 'til Sarah stops playing with her hair and showing off her boots and finds the right page. Then I hear a sweet little Tinkerbell voice, sliding up out of my throat like drool off Skippy's tongue. "I like your boots."

Sarah pulls one black boot up onto her knee and unzips it. "I've got brown ones, too," she says. "Wanna' try one on? They're real vinyl. Those sneakers hand-me-downs from your cousin?"

I tuck my white sneakers in under my desk and nod. Before Sarah gets her boot all the way off, Miss Creelman marches down the aisle, her Kurly Kate hair bouncing. Even her armpit hair is orange. Not like I even wanted to know that, but she wears shells a lot so you can't help but notice. "Now, girls. This is reading time, not fashion runway time."

"Sorry, Miss Creelman." But after the teacher's gone, Sarah sticks her thumbs in her ears and waggles her fingers behind Miss Creelman's back.

At lunchtime on Wednesday, I find a place far away from everybody under the horse chestnut tree where Bren and me used to build Troll towns. I get Frodo out of my pocket and start making a cottage for him out of sticks and acorns and chestnut shells. Melody's the only one close to me, but she's busy collecting chestnuts and not paying any attention to me. I'm so busy trying to get the leaf roof to stay on my house that I don't notice the girls behind me. Until I look up to see where the sun got to.

"Whatcha' doin', Blinky? Playing house?"

My heart starts galloping. One of Sarah's shiny black boots is real close to the wall I just finished.

"What's with the fat naked hippie doll with the smucked-in nose and red eyes? He a pregnant retard?"

Like some kind of whispery echo, Penny says, "Yeah, is he a retard doll?"

"He's a Troll," I mumble to the ground ... *And that's not a very nice word, and only girls can get pregnant, and did you forget I'm the best reader in the whole class?* My eye's twitching and my voice's got the shimmy shake it gets when I want to hide.

"Looks like flippin' Junior Tattrie, with his gorilla face," Sarah says. "What's he so darn happy about? He's ugly."

I shrug and grin up at her.

"Want me to help?" she asks.

"Sure," I say. "Can't get the stupid roof to stay on."

Only instead of bending down beside me, Sarah keeps

standing. Tries to grab hold of me with her eye-lock. "I'll be the rich guy that owns the wrecking ball company."

I'm still trying to figure out what she's talking about when the earth starts shaking. I scramble to hold up the walls of my Troll house. The bump only lasts a few seconds, but soon as it's done, Sarah starts swinging her boot, back and forth, back and forth. Acorns and dirt, sticks and stones fly everywhere. I snatch Frodo away just before the wrecking ball gets to him.

My bad eye slams shut.

I want to shove Sarah ...

Into outer space.

But I'm frozen stiff. Except for my dirty fingers crawling up into my mouth.

"Why did you do that?" Her voice is so quiet, I have to check to make sure Melody's lips are moving. She's standing up, and she's got one small hand on Sarah's arm. "She worked on it all recess."

Sarah gives one last kick, then brushes off her jacket sleeve. "Keep your filthy hands off me, you germy freak. You dirty Indian." Then she stretches her fish lips wide open so it looks like she swallowed her whole entire head. "Look! You ripped my new jacket!"

"Where?" We all stare at the sleeve of Sarah's red and black plaid jacket.

The jacket I wanted for my birthday and didn't get.

"Not there, you little dog turds. Here."

Sure enough, there's a tiny hole in her other sleeve.

Looks to me like a cigarette burn. Probably from Her Royal Lowness.

"I think it was your other arm I touched," Melody whispers.

Sarah whips around. Puts both hands on Melody's chest and shoves her. Hard. Melody trips over the slide and slams onto her bum on her prickly pile of horse chestnuts. One of her rubber boots flies off. When she looks up, her brown eyes are all wet and shiny, like tadpoles.

"I'm telling My Mother!" Sarah turns and looks at Penny and Vickie. "She paid $29.95 for ..."

Melody gets on her hands and knees, pushes herself up. Scoops up a big handful of wet muddy leaves and spiky chestnut shells, shoves her foot back in her boot, then climbs up onto the bottom of the slide, behind Sarah.

" ... this jacket." Sarah turns back to face Melody. "And you better hope My Mother doesn't find out it's you been stealing stuff ... wha ...?"

Melody grabs Sarah behind the head. Grinds the leaves and shells into her face.

Hard.

Like she's juicing an orange.

Penny sucks in a bunch of air, and the other girls all step back.

Junior and Wade come sniffing over with their hound dog noses. "Cat fight! Cat fight!"

I stand up and wipe the dirt off Frodo, but I don't say

a word. I'm pretty sure everybody can hear my heart thumping. See my legs shaking.

"Ooooh! Ohhhh! You maniac! You crazy Indian!" Sarah tries to wipe the mud off her face and her hair. "Well, don't just stand there. Somebody help me!"

While Sarah's still spitting and hissing like a cornered cat, the bell goes. Melody beats it for the door and lines up.

I stuff Frodo in my pocket and walk slowly behind her. My whole body's shaking from laughing on the inside and being scared poopless, all at the same time.

When Sarah finally comes back to class, she's got some nasty red scratches on her nose and cheeks, and the purple snake's squirming around in her forehead again. I look up every time Miss Creelman walks by Melody's desk, wait for the teacher to lean in and hiss into Melody's ear. But she doesn't.

I keep my head down and work on my math, like long division's the most interesting thing since television.

I'm almost finished the chapter when somebody knocks on the door, just before the three o'clock bell. The door creaks open and Mr. Grant strides into the classroom.

Melody slides down in her seat and stares at her desk.

The principal's got on his black overcoat, with his long umbrella hooked over one arm. With his white shirt collar all buttoned up and no necktie, he looks like a minister. He whispers something to Miss Creelman, then waggles his finger for Melody to come to the front of the room.

She starts shivering and rubbing her arms. Slips out of

her seat, stands up, and shuffles up the aisle. Keeps her eyes on the floor. Mr. Grant leans over and says something to her that I can't hear, then reaches out to her. She jerks her shoulder away, jams her hands into the pockets of Sarah's old green jumper, then follows him out into the hall. Miss Creelman closes the door behind them.

The classroom goes quiet, like July. Will we hear the strap all the way from the office?

Melody comes back just as the bell rings. She's not crying and her hands don't look red at all. One cheek's all bulged out, like she's got a jawbreaker stuffed inside. Did it come from Mr. Grant's emergency candy drawer? The one right beside the strap drawer?

She bends over to put her books away under her seat, looks up through her long lashes at me, and smiles. Reaches out her closed hand, then turns it over so I can see what she's got. She nods her head, points her eyes at the candy. I smile back, reach out, take the shiny black jawbreaker, pop it into my mouth, then look over my shoulder. Sarah's glaring at me, trying to get me in her eye-lock. I turn back around, swallow some sweet licorice juice, and make myself busy trying to find something in my desk.

Nanny's in the kitchen peeling apples when I get home. "Your mother and the baby are having a check-up with Doc Murray. You got some mail."

"I did? From Bren?" I take the postcard, help myself to an oatmeal cookie, and sit down at the kitchen table across from Nanny.

Hi Jenn:

I'm sending you this postcard from Prince Edward Island! Karen's family took me to visit Woodleigh Replicas—that's where these little castles are. My first time on the ferry boat and I didn't get seasick! Sorry I didn't get to visit you in the summer. Mom says maybe I can next year.

Yours truly, Bren

But *we* were going to go to P.E.I. together; Bren and me. On the ferry boat.

"Hear there's a family of Indians moved to town," Nanny says. "You're not associating with them, are you?"

I stand the postcard up on the windowsill, the side with the perfect little castles facing out. "Well, there's a new girl in my class. Melody Syliboy. I don't know her much, but she's a good reader and she's got pretty hair."

"Humph. Don't let them fool you. Turn your back and they'll be robbing you blind. First it was my blanket, now your grampy's plaid jacket's gone missing from the barn."

"I don't think Melody's family lives out near you," I say.

"Makes no difference. They're quiet and sneaky—most likely come when they know I'm sleeping. Taking advantage of an old lady that's hard of hearing."

"The other girls are being mean to her. Not the other way around. Same as they're mean to me. I feel sorry for her."

"Stick with your own kind's my best advice. Now, get changed out of your good school clothes. We've got some wood to split after I'm done these apple dumplings."

"I've been practicing with the hatchet. I'm almost as good a chopper as Dad, now."

Nanny looks over top her glasses at me. Lifts her eyebrows. "Somebody's been helping their self to my woodpile. I've got to get the loan of some from your dad, hold me over 'til I can get another load delivered."

"Did the thief leave you another surprise, like the twig basket?" I ask.

She snorts. "You could say that—a rabbit carcass. Had to skin it myself, but it did make a nice stew. I put some in the fridge for your father's supper."

Dear Bren:

Thank you for the castle postcard. Wish I could go to PEI.

Sarah's still sweet as maple sugar one minute, sour as chokecherries the next. Melody stood right up to her at school. Smucked some prickly horse chestnut shells right into her face. And she didn't even get the strap! Mr. Grant took it easy on her since she's new. She gave me a candy.

Wish I was brave like that. Melody might be more like the wild Indians at Nanny's old school than I thought. Or maybe she's just sick and tired of Sarah being mean. I wish everybody knew the Golden Rule, like the Girl of the Limberlost, Elnora. Do unto others as you would have them do unto you, which sounds like Bible talk but means treat everybody the way you want them to treat you. Did you get to read it?

The mystery's still going on because somebody took wood from Nanny's woodpile and Grampy's barn jacket's missing too. Don't know why anybody would want that old thing.

I hope there's no mean girls at your school.

I miss you.

Your friend, Jenn

CHAPTER 9

(WHEREIN Jennifer Plays Pirates)

Saturday morning, I get up early and re-read two chapters of *The Girl of the Limberlost*. Elnora sure knows a lot about butterflies, caterpillars, and moths. Dad told me it was plants from swamps like the Limberlost that turned into coal, ages ago. Doesn't make a bit of sense to me since plants are mostly green and pretty and coal's black and ugly. And stinky.

Mom and Dad are busy painting the kitchen cupboards. I read part of *The Gingerbread Man* to Bethy. When she gets cranky and starts trying to eat the book, I put her in the playpen for her morning nap, then go out to the shed to see what there is to make a net. Dad's got two different ones for fishing, but the holes are too big for butterflies. I find one of the bamboo stakes Mom uses for her tomato plants, then look around for something to use for the net part.

Mom and Dad are having a tea break when I go back inside. I plug my nose. "Pee-ew! That paint stinks. Do we have anything I can use to make a butterfly net?"

"Why on earth would you want to catch butterflies?" Mom blows on her tea, then takes a sip. "They belong outdoors."

"I just want to study them," I say. "I'm not going to kill them, stick them on cork boards or anything. I'll just watch them for a while, then let them go."

She roots around in the junk drawer. "I think I've got some old cheesecloth in here somewhere, left over from making apple jelly. Aha! This piece big enough?"

I spread the see-through white material out on the kitchen table. "Should be. Now I've just gotta figure out what I can use for the circle part."

"There's some copper wire on my workbench," Dad says. "The wire snips are hanging right above it. Watch you don't pinch your fingers."

I get the net all put together, then sit on the steps watching the glue dry. I'm impatient, but I make myself wait for the church bells to ring again. Mom's old straw gardening hat's hanging by the shed door, so I put it on, tie the pink scarf under my chin, just like Elnora. Only she plays the violin, makes it sound like all the swamp creatures. "Song of the Limberlost" she calls it. I don't have a violin, but I can sing; I'll call it "Song of the Pit Pond."

Come take up your hats, and away let us haste,
to the Butterfly's ball and the Grasshopper's feast ...
And there was the Gnat and the Dragonfly, too,
with all their relations, green, orange and blue ...

Still can't figure out what a gnat is. Finally the church bells ring ten times. I pick up the net and run around the yard with it, to make sure it won't fall apart. Then I get on my bike, stick the net in my basket, and pull up by the back step. I ring my bell and shout in through the screen door. "Just going down to the Pit Pond."

Skippy woofs, then prances around on his back legs. "Nope. Don't think the butterflies would much like you and your sniffing and barking."

Except for the birds, it's quiet when I get there. I lean my bike up against a tree trunk, then put my net over one shoulder and stroll around the pond. Listen to the swamp music: the bees buzzing, the crickets and grasshoppers chirping. A big old turtle's sunning himself on a stone along one edge. I duck when two dragonflies zoom past my head—devil's darning needles, Nanny calls them. Is September too cold for butterflies? Maybe they're already hibernating like bears, waiting for spring.

I look up when I hear somebody shouting. Junior and Wade are running around over by where the number two and number four mines used to be. The old mine pitheads got all sealed up after the Big Bump. Flooded, then filled with cement so nobody falls in. The Bad Boys are having

a swordfight, and Junior's got a black patch over one eye.
Maybe Wade binged him with a rock.

Through the big windows on the old brick lantern
building, where the miners used to pick up their head
lamps, I see somebody else. Skipping. Even from way over
here, I can hear her singing. A song we did in choir last year.

Land of the silver birch,
home of the beaver;
where still the mighty moose
wanders at will.
Blue lake and rocky shore,
I will return once ...

Wade and Junior spot Melody when she gets to the corner.
"Injun!" Wade shouts. "Let's get her!"

Melody takes off running. Car tires squeal when she
dashes across the road, her long hair flying out behind her
like a cape. "Hey! Watch where you're going!" the driver
shouts out the window. "You tryin' to get yourself killed?"

Melody doesn't slow down, disappears into the woods
out back of the pond. The Bad Boys try to hide their swords
behind their backs and smile at the man in the car. Junior's
even whistling.

I walk fast around the edge of the pond, look back over
my shoulder 'til I can't see the Bad Boys anymore. I look
out underneath the brim of my hat, up at the trees and the
wispy white clouds puffing like train smoke across the blue

sky. Jack Frost's already been to visit; most of the flowers are crunchy and brown, and the tall brown cattails are leaking fur all over the place. Sometime over the summer, a giant pointy pine tree must've got hit by lightning. It's burnt black where it snapped in two, and the long part's stretched out over the pond, like a bridge. I sit on the splintery end of it, make sure the Bad Boys can't see me, then stare out over the top of the pond. There's no breeze, so most of it's like a mirror, only with little puckers every time a dragonfly darts down to snatch a bug up out of the water. It's so quiet and still, it's spooky. When the bushes start rustling behind me, I jerk my head around.

There isn't any wind.

Is somebody watching me?

I look back out over the pond and start singing softly. "Land of the silver birch, home of the beaver ..." Something catches my eye, way down at the floating tip-top of the burnt tree. Something big and pale green. Clinging to a prickly branch, gently fluttering its wings open and closed, open and closed, like it's dancing. Is it a Luna moth? I've never seen a real one before, only in books. But, shouldn't it be sleeping in the daytime? I stand up, put one foot on the tree, then the other, and inch sideways along the thick trunk to get a closer look.

I reach my net out in front of me, but the big moth's still too far away. Looks almost as big as my hand. I shuffle sideways along the tree a little further, bend my knees and hold my arms out to keep my balance.

"That your grandmother's Easter bonnet?"

I glance back over my shoulder. Junior and Wade are standing at the other end of the tree bridge. Wade's whacking the fuzzy tops off the cattails with his wooden sword.

I turn to face the Luna moth again. Put my arms down by my sides so I don't look scared. My eye's twitching.

"Hey, I know," Wade says. "Let's make her walk the plank!"

"Ahoy, Matey. Jolly good idea," Junior says.

I look down at the water, at the yellow and brown leaves stuck to it, and my eye slams shut. With my good eye, I watch the Luna moth flutter up into the sky, then disappear above the treetops.

I hunker down when the tree starts jiggling; they're jumping up and down on it, waving their swords around, stabbing them in the air as they walk toward me. "Get moving!" Junior shouts. "Walk the plank, you one-eyed devil!"

The murky brown water splashes up around where the tree's hitting it. Dad says the pond's bottomless because there's miles of mine tunnels underneath. A perfect hiding place for the Breath Grabber.

"Arrg ... Maybe she's got some booty for us," Wade says. "What's that you've got, girl?"

All of a sudden, the ground starts grumbling and shaking; the top of the pond gets all ripply, like somebody threw a bunch of stones into it. I grab onto one of the needly pine branches to keep from falling in.

When the bump's over, Junior laughs his burr prickle head off. "What's wrong, Blinky? Not scared of gettin' wet, are you?"

Wade's close enough now to poke me in the bum with his sword. "Not scared of a little water, are you, girl?" *Poke, poke, poke.*

I inch further away from them, closer to the skinny end of the tree. Cold water seeps into my sneakers. I freeze when a warbly bird call wobbles all around me. Like the loons on Sandy Bottom Lake.

"Move it!" Junior bounces harder, like he's on Mr. MacLeod's trampoline.

The wet bark's slippery. I drop my net and grab onto a branch, but it snaps off in my hands. I wave my arms around in the air, try to catch my balance. Wade gives me one good jab with his sword.

And I fall.

Backwards.

Smack into the pond's icy water.

I splash around, frantically grabbing at the branches, the lily pads, anything. "Help!" I scream. "I can't swim!"

But the Bad Boys are gone.

I suck in a big dirty mouthful of water, close my eyes, and go under. Sink like an anchor. Water shoots up my nose, blasts into my ears. I drop down, deep down, into the Breath Grabber's cave. He grabs onto me, squeezes my middle, squishes the breath right out of me. White stars flash inside my eyelids. I try to squint my eyes open, only the water's too muddy to see anything.

But the pond's not bottomless! My sneakers touch bottom, oozy, swampy bottom.

I bend my knees, try to push off, but the muck's like quicksand. Sucking up my sneakers. Something grabs my leg. Then my other leg. Is it the Breath Grabber? For real? Something else wiggles in under my armpits. My eyes pop open, and I look behind me.

Not a monster. A person. Somebody with long dark hair floating all around them. I blink. Am I seeing double? It's Melody, only there's two of her. I shake my head, then flop over like a rag doll and let myself be dragged up through the dirty water, back to the sparkling sun.

She pulls me up by my arms, out of the pond and up the bank. I collapse on my belly on the grass, coughing and choking, spitting out mucky water and trying to breathe.

When I finally sit up, Melody's face is full of worry wrinkles. "Are you okay?"

"The Bad Boys. They ... made me ... walk the plank." I pull off my sopping wet hat and look around. "But there were two of you. Down in the water. Weren't there?"

She shakes her head. "You were panicking."

"But I'm bigger than you. How could you be strong enough to pull me out?"

"I'm a good swimmer." She stuffs her bare feet back into her rubber boots. "Remember?"

"Sure felt like four hands down there," I insist.

A car horn toots, and I turn around and look at the street

behind us.

A police car's pulled up next to the curb, and Officer Mills is just opening the door. "Everything all right there?" he calls over the roof. "Is that you, Jennifer?"

"Yes, sir. Everything's fine," I shout. "Just an accident. I got a little wet but I'm going home now."

"No swimming allowed in the Pit Pond," he says.

"Yes, sir." I smile and wave and he gets back in his car. When I turn back around, Melody's sitting on a boulder, wringing the water out of her hair.

"Last time I told on them, Junior chased me home from school every day for a week. Never caught me, though."

Melody jumps down and picks up my soggy hat. "Want me to walk home with you?"

I stand up and shiver. "I'm freezing, but it's not far."

We walk toward my bike. "Oh, my net," I say. "I almost caught a Luna moth."

She smiles. "Like Elnora Comstock. My mom says seeing a Luna moth means one of your ancestors is paying you a visit."

"Really? Looked more like a fairy than my grampy."

We look back along the pine tree and in the water around it. There's no sign of my net.

"The Bad Boys better not catch any butterflies with it," I say. "They'd most likely torture them."

"They're so stupid. Didn't they think you might drown?"

"Well, Wade's supposed to be in Grade 7. As Nanny says,

if clues were shoes, he'd be barefoot. Get it?"

Melody nods and we both laugh. I push my bike out to Main Street, and we walk back toward uptown. We're giggling at the fart sounds my sneakers are making when a noisy engine rumbles up behind us. Somebody honks the horn and we both turn around.

"It's my Nanny!"

Nanny pulls her old gray half-ton up to the curb, then leans over and rolls down the window. "Kind of a cool day for a dip, isn't it, Jennifer?"

"I got pushed." My bottom lip wobbles and I bite it to keep from crying. "Into the Pit Pond. Can you give us a ride home? Me and Melody?"

Nanny looks hard at Melody, at her long soaking-wet black hair, then frowns, jerks her thumb at her. "Humph. Was it her pushed you in?"

"No. Somebody else." I frown back at her. "Can you help me get my bike in the back? Please?"

Nanny turns off the truck, gets out, opens the rusty tailgate, and we lift my bike in. She squints over top her glasses at Melody. "You can ride in the back. Don't want to get my seats too dirty."

Melody looks down at the road. "That's all right, ma'am. I'll walk."

"I'll ride in the back with you, Melody. You rescued me," I say. "You'll get sick walking around soaking wet like that."

But she's already gone. Walking over the bridge, up McGee Road toward the prison.

"Well, shut the door. Don't have all day, you know," Nanny says. "Told you there'd be nothing but trouble you start gettin' in with the Indians."

I roll my window down when we drive past Melody. "Thank you," I yell. "See you at school Monday." Only I don't think she can hear me with Nanny grinding the gears.

After supper, I find Mom in the living room having a tea time-out and singing to Bethy; "God Sees the Little Sparrow Fall," Number 588 in the navy-blue hymnbook. I sing, too.

> *God sees the little sparrow fall,*
> *It meets His tender view;*
> *If God so loves the little birds,*
> *I know He loves me, too.*

Bethy's sitting in her little yellow ducky chair, kicking her feet and cooing along.

"You sure you don't want me to call the Tattries and the Skidmores?" Mom's using her belly like a TV tray to hold her teacup. Even though Beth was born right before last Christmas, looks like part of her's still in there. Mom didn't have time to get a perm since then, so her brownish-red hair's flat and flyaway, like mine. She looks more like herself with curly hair and no belly.

"Yes! I mean, no! You didn't, did you?"

She shakes her head.

"They'd be even meaner to me if I tattled," I say.

"Lucky for you there was somebody around to save you."

"Mmmm ..." I bunch up my shoulders and use the jagged edge of my chewed-up thumbnail to scrape my bottom teeth. "Do you know the Syliboys?"

Mom stares at my mouth. The *Nibble No More* she got for my nails tastes like turpentine smells, only I keep licking it off anyway. I yank my thumb out and pick Frodo up off the coffee table.

"Not really. I met her mother at the P.T.A. meeting. She certainly seems very nice." Mom presses her lips together and sighs. "Janet Pearo up at the hospital said Mrs. Syliboy did her nurse's training at the Aberdeen, but there's no work here so she's getting some housekeeping hours up at the prison."

"Is Melody an only child?" I ask.

Mom shrugs. "I'm not sure, but I know they've had more than their fair share of troubles." She scrunches her faded end-of-day orange lips up into a whistle shape and blows on her tea, then takes a sip. "Ooh! That's hot. One of the ladies in my church group thought she heard that Mr. Syliboy passed away recently."

Passed away.

PASSED AWAY.

The words bounce around in my brain. I stop braiding Frodo's hair and stare at her. "Geez! Like Elnora Comstock's father. How old was he?"

She frowns. "Don't take the name of the Lord in vain, Jennifer."

"I wasn't." I wrap Frodo's long blue hair around my pointer finger. "Geez is just the same as gee whiz, only I've got lazy lips."

I pick Bethy up and give her a horsey ride on my knee. "Da da dum da da dum da da dum dum dum ... Except for in books, I thought only old people died. Like Grampy and Great Uncle Bernie. Not people's fathers."

Mom shakes her head. "I suppose that's most often the case, but accidents and illness can happen to anybody anytime. Don't forget the Big Bump."

"Oh, yeah." I close my eyes and nuzzle my nose into Bethy's soft neck. She makes her little cooing sound.

I never knew anybody with a dead father before.

What was she doing when the rest of us were making Father's Day cards?

"I'll bet Melody could really use a friend, being the only new girl at school and all." Mom puts her arm around my shoulders. We make a Bethy sandwich. "Is she a nice girl?"

I nod, but I can't squeeze any words out. Sarah's rat-nose keeps stabbing into my brain.

"Jenn?"

Bethy's getting squirmy, so I get up and put her in her playpen. She uses the rail to pull herself up and starts trying to climb out. "Sarah says Melody's a dirty wild Indian," I blurt out. "Her mother told her."

Mom sits up straight, splashes some tea onto her skirt. "Nonsense!" She uses a corner of Bethy's flannel burp blanket to mop up the tea. "Melody may be a Native person, but that does not make her any dirtier than anybody else. It's a crying shame that some people think that way."

"She doesn't look dirty," I say. "Or wild. And she's got real pretty hair and maple taffy skin."

Mom breathes out a long, tired sigh that smells like tea. "Oh, Jenny." She shakes her head. "It's best to be color-blind. When it comes to people, that is. Every single one of us is equal in God's eyes."

I lean down, put my nose up to Bethy's and stare cross-eyed into her big blue eyes. She giggles and grabs my nose. "Not in Sarah's eyes," I say. "Or Nanny's."

"Fortunately, Sarah Saunders and your grandmother are not in charge of the world. Although they both might like to think they are." Mom sets her tea down and brushes my bangs out of my eyes. "Why don't you invite Melody over sometime?"

"Maybe. She likes the same kind of books as me. And I think she likes to sing."

"She must live out on Herrett Road, does she? Saw her standing in the pasture across from the prison field yesterday. Looked like she was waving to somebody."

"I dunno."

Dad and me watch *The Lone Ranger* before bed. Melody does look like Tonto. But she doesn't talk all jerky like him. *Kemosabe want Tonto find Silver? Silver good horse. Almost good as Scout.* When the show's over, I tiptoe upstairs so I don't wake Bethy up. Pull my cozy quilt up over my head and practice my scales for a while. I'm trying to get above high C, but I haven't made it up past "A" yet. Miss Dill calls it "singing over the bridge." My bridge is still too high for my voice to climb over.

When Dad comes to tuck me in, I practically strangle him with my hug.

"What's that for?"

I let go, then plant a big smacker on his sandpaper cheek. "Just because."

Dear Bren:

The Bad Boys almost drowned me today when I was trying to catch a Luna Moth. It was the scariest thing that ever happened to me. I don't ever want to die. The new girl saved me. When I was under the water I saw two people with long black hair but she said she was by herself. Melody's a lot nicer than some girls. I think she likes to sing too. Maybe I'll ask her over to play sometime.

If you're not too busy having fun with Karen could you please write back to me?

Your Friend,

Jenn

CHAPTER 10

(WHEREIN Miss Dill Acts as Matchmaker)

Last week of September, Miss Dill tells us about the Miners' Hall Concert. "As most of you know, Springhill has an anniversary concert in support of the Miners' Hall every October," she says. "This year marks the tenth anniversary of the Big Bump. Now that you're in Grade 5, you may participate as performers. Our Grade 5 and 6 choir will sing one or two songs, but if you would like to perform by yourself or with a friend, please speak to me sometime before the end of the week."

Sarah shoots her arm up and waves her hand around in the air.

"After class, please, Sarah. Now, who remembers our articulation warm-up exercises from last year?"

Nobody puts up their hand.

"Jennifer—surely you remember one of them?"

I blush, but my head nods up and down anyway. "The lips, the teeth, the tip of the tongue," I whisper.

"A little louder, Jennifer. Let your angel's voice sing out!"

I repeat it, only louder, so she'll move on to somebody else.

Then I hear Melody's voice. She's standing right next to me in the front row. "A big black bug bit a big black bear, and the big black bear bled blood."

Everybody giggles.

Miss Dill beams. "Perfect. Some new material! Thank you, Melody, for your contribution."

When the recess bell goes, Miss Dill asks Melody and me to stay back. "I could hear your two voices above all the others," she says. "They complement each other so beautifully. I'd be delighted to help you prepare a duet for the Concert, if you'd like."

My bad eye starts twitching, and I put my thumbnail between my front teeth.

Melody stares at the floor and twists her hair around her pointer finger.

"Ah ... I see. I used to have an awful problem with nerves," Miss Dill says. "I can teach you a few secrets, if you'd like. About where to put your eyes and your mind to keep your nerves from acting up. Beautiful singing voices like yours are heavenly gifts meant to be shared." She turns and picks up one of Melody's hands. "How are you settling in, Melody? Is there anything I can do to help you? Anything at all?"

Melody blushes and jerks her hand away, then whispers, "No, thank you, Miss."

Miss Dill frowns and pauses for a second. "Well, promise me you'll think about it, at least," she says. "You both sing like angels, and I think your voices would sound glorious harmonizing."

"Do you like singing?" Melody asks when we get out in the hallway.

I nod. "It's my favorite thing. I want to be a singer when I grow up."

"Me, too."

"What kind of music do you like?" I ask.

"Mostly country and western," she says. "And church music."

"I like Annie Murray," I say. "She's from Springhill and she used to keep house for us. She's on television. *Singalong Jubilee.*"

"We don't have television."

"We only got a black and white one last year," I say. "We've got a record player, too, and I've got my own transistor radio in my room."

"We've just got the big radio in the kitchen," she says.

"I want to be on *Singalong Jubilee* when I'm big." I hold the heavy hall door open for her. "Like Annie. Or maybe even *The Ed Sullivan Show.*"

"Who's Ed Sullivan?" she asks.

I gawk at her. "You don't know who Ed Sullivan is? He's only got the biggest show on TV ... 'a really big shew,' he always says. Mostly he's got famous singers on, like the Beatles and Elvis, but one time he had some of the Springhill miners on his show."

"I'd like to see it," she says.

"Maybe Mom'll let you come watch with us," I say. "It's on Sunday nights."

At lunchtime Thursday, I talk to Melody about Elnora while I'm putting on my jacket. We're giggling like Bren and me used to, until Sarah grabs my arm on the way down the hall and whispers, "Melody Silly Boy Germs," loud enough so everybody can hear.

I shake off her hand and mumble, "I'm not playing." Melody puts her head down and keeps walking.

"Well, don't have a conniption." Sarah puts her pinchy face right up next to mine so I can smell the Tang she had for breakfast and see her orange moustache. She's got three red pimples on her forehead. "*All* the girls are playing."

I look at the other girls behind her and my eye starts twitching. "I ... I ... I didn't mean ... It's just that ... well ... Melody's new. She's got no friends."

"Of course she doesn't." Sarah puts her hands on her hips. "She's a dirty Indian."

I look down the hall. At the swish of long black hair disappearing between the heavy front doors.

"And Blinky?"

I squint back at Sarah.

She's got her arms crossed and she's grinning like the

Alice in Wonderland cat again. "Don't you *want* to be in the Hip Hive? Now that Brenda's not here to be your only friend?"

My eye slams shut, then I turn around and run outside.

Melody's got her hood up and she's hugging herself. When she gets to the horse chestnut tree, she flops down against it. Her taffy face disappears into her brown plaid arms.

The playground gets real quiet. The only sound's the girls buzzing around the Queen Bee behind me.

Takes me about an hour to get to the tree. I cough, then scuff the toe of my sneaker against the gray roots and kick away some spiky chestnuts. After another hour of scuffing and kicking, Melody tucks her hair behind one ear and peeks out at me with her Bambi eyes.

My belly drops. Plops right down between my legs. Same as when we drive past a raccoon mashed into the highway.

I rub my bad eye, then dig a wrinkly pink Kleenex out of my jacket pocket. "It's not used ... I don't think."

She stands up, takes the Kleenex, chews on her bottom lip, and tries to smile. "Thanks. Want a bite?" While she wipes her eyes, we take turns nibbling on her ginger cookie.

After a while, Melody bends down and picks up a split green chestnut pocket. "It's a double. Twins are real good luck. Want half?"

I crouch down beside her and stare at the treasure.

"Really? Never heard tell of that before. Do we make a wish?"

She shakes her head. "No. We each keep half, and then we'll be lucky together."

I shrug, then stick out my hand and she gives me one of the chestnuts. The biggest one. I whistle and polish it up with my thumb. "It's a beauty! Thanks." I stuff it into my jacket pocket.

The fire whistle blows and the bell rings at the same time, so I can't make out what she's saying when we walk across the parking lot and up the cement steps together. But I smile and nod, like it's real interesting. And make like I don't feel the girls' sharp eyes poking me in the back.

In bed at night, I hug my old monkey, Cheeky, hard. Chew on his rubber banana and stare out my window at the twinkly black sky around my pointy pine tree. *One, two, three, four ...* After fifty, I lose track of what stars I already counted. The boringest song I can think of is "The Twelve Days of Christmas," so I whisper-sing it all the way through to the twelve lords-a-leaping, two times.

When the ten o'clock church chimes go, I'm still wide awake like the night before Christmas.

Melody doesn't show up at school Friday morning.

At recess, I stay in to clean the long-division problems off the blackboard. When I lean out to bang the chalk brushes together, I hum "Puff" and practice my whistling so I can't hear the "MSG" screams blasting in through the window.

"Sounds like they're having lots of fun playing that new

game," Miss Creelman says. "I wonder how it goes?"

I cough through the cloud of yellow chalk dust and think about trying to explain it to her. What would she say if I told her the other girls were treating Melody like a germ?

Like the measles or the mumps?

Would she even believe me?

Could she make them stop?

I'm just about to open my mouth when she says, "Isn't it nice the way all the children in our class get along so well?"

I close my mouth, slam the window shut, wipe my chalky hands on my gray jumper. And nod.

CHAPTER 11

(WHEREIN Jennifer Gets Itchy)

Saturday morning, I wake up with bigger problems than Sarah Saunders. Both my eyeballs hurt when I try to open them. My bad one stays shut. All my hairs hurt, too, even the little blonde ones you can't hardly see on my arms. My head feels like a giant sack of potatoes, and I'm freezing and roasting all at the same time.

I wiggle my sore feet into my fuzzy blue slippers and shuffle downstairs. When I plop my twenty-pound potato head down, the kitchen table feels like ice on my hot cheek. But only for one breath. "I'm sick," I try to say. Only it comes out like a groan.

Mom sets Beth down in her bouncy chair, then puts one cool hand on my forehead.

"Heavens to Murgatroyd! You're burning up, Jenn. You

go straight back to bed. I'll bring you up some ice water and an aspirin after I feed Bethy." She pats me on the bum.

I make an ouch face and shuffle back upstairs. Pile up my books on my orange crate nightstand, then crawl back into bed with Cheeky.

By the time Mom makes it upstairs, I'm so hot I can't talk right. "Hi, Muzzy. I sick—you make all better?" I giggle, but I have to shut my mouth when she pops the thermometer in.

She leaves it stabbing into the roof of my mouth for about an hour. I hardly dare swallow so I won't get poisoned from the silver stuff inside the glass. Finally, she takes it out, holds it up to the window to read, then shakes her head. "A hundred and three! No wonder you're so warm. Let's try some aspirin and a bath."

I suck on the pink Loveheart baby aspirin and fall back asleep while she's running the water. By the time the tub's full, my pillowcase is soaked like one of Bethy's diapers. Only not so smelly.

I reach out and stick a shaky finger into the bath water. "Is it b ... b ... boiling?"

"Medium," Mom says. "Give it a try. I'm just going to change Beth."

I giggle and do a pee shiver. "Can you change her into a b ... b ... bunny, just for today, a soft gray one with a p ... p ... pink nose?"

She smiles and closes the bathroom door.

I keep adding hot water, and then Mom finally comes back and pulls me out of the tub. "You're as floppy as a sock monkey. Quick like a bunny, now." She wraps me up in a big soft pink towel and rubs me dry. When I get back in bed, my teeth are clacking together like typewriter keys. The typewriter bell's even clanging. When my bad eye slams shut, I figure I'll close the other one, too, just for a sec. Sounds like Mom's talking to me real slow through a long cardboard tube. Is she speaking Pig Latin?

Mom and Dad come in to look at me sometime after dark. Maybe I'm asleep. Sounds like they're at the bottom of Nanny's old stone well, only I can still hear them if I listen hard and don't breathe.

"Hope it's not the chickenpox," Mom whispers. "Mike's kids had it just after we saw them at the family reunion."

I was deaf all of February from an ear infection, until my eardrum broke and slimy green pus poured out. Now I've gotta get chickenpox, too?

"But wasn't that three weeks ago?" Dad says.

"Maybe it's going around the ..." But I fall asleep before she finishes her sentence.

"Amazing grace, how sweet the sound ..." Dad puts down his guitar and turns away from me. Wings! Why does he have wings? I look down—there's something white and fluffy swirling around my legs. Only it's warm, so it's not snow. Are they clouds? I run to try and catch up with Dad, only he flies away. I look around—everybody's flying—except me. "Dad!" I shout, but nobody can hear me.

Except for one old man with a long list in his hand. "Were you calling me, dear?" he says. "Most people call me Father, but occasionally I get called Dad." He looks down at his list. "Welcome to my Kingdom, but aren't you a little early? I don't see your name ..."

"King God!" I jerk awake, but even with my eyes open I can't erase the picture of angel Dad from my mind. I get up to pee. My mouth tastes like I had sand for supper, so I brush my teeth. My gums feel all bruisey, like I imagine they'd feel if somebody punched me in the mouth.

I crouch down by my window and watch Dad walk down the driveway and get into Old Red. *Phew!* No wings. I smile and climb back into bed and pull the covers up over my head. Mom does her best to tiptoe in. Only the floor creaks.

"You awake, Jenny?" she whispers.

I try to open my eyes, but my bad one's still slammed shut.

"Just push your blankets back for a sec, sweetie," Mom says. "And lift up your PJ top."

The whole world turns into the Tilt-a-Whirl when I try to sit up. When the spinning finally lets up, we both take a real good gander at my belly. Besides some sleep wrinkles, my outsy bellybutton and all look about the same as always.

"Thank goodness. Must just be the flu," she says, like the flu is the funnest thing in the whole entire world, which isn't exactly the way I remember it from last year.

"But my hair still hurts, and my head's itchy, like I've got fleas." I reach up and scratch the top of my head. What's that goop? If I was outside, I'd think it was bird poop. I look at my slimy fingers, then smell them. My nose holes pop open and my top lip curls up. "Yuck."

"Let me see. Sit up straight and bend over." She grabs onto my head with both hands, like she's looking for nits. At least my head only feels like a small sack of potatoes today, only my hairs still hurt, every last one of them.

"Oh, shoot. It must be the chickenpox." She looks so upset, I want to hug her, but I'm still floppy as a sock monkey. Her sad Skippy eyes watch me get my sore self back into my nest.

"What about all the yucky cod liver oil pills I take at school? Aren't they supposed to keep me from getting sick?"

Mom laughs. "They're just to give you Vitamin D since we don't get much sunshine around here outside of July and August."

"So, how do we get rid of these chickens? Find a fox? Good job it's only a couple."

She pulls the blankets up under my chin. "Time. Time's the only thing that gets rid of the chickenpox, Jenn. And, believe you me, there's no such thing as having only a couple. You'll be spotted like a leopard by suppertime."

"Can I watch television all day? Is it time for *Mr. Dressup*?"

"Let's try some cereal, then we'll talk about it."

"Do we have any Pop Tarts?"

"Could be. I'll go downstairs and check."

Only she comes back with a boring bowl of Fluffs. She tries to bend her mouth up into a smile, but her eyes look too tired. "Sorry, Jenn. I think I need to take a nap when I put Bethy down for hers."

She pushes her hair away from her pale face and closes her eyes. "I feel a bit faint. Must be the heat. I know it'll be hard, but you should stay away from Bethy, just until the pox dry up. Chickenpox can be dangerous for little babies."

"What about for big girls?" I ask.

She shakes her head. "You'll be itchy, hot, and feverish for a few days, but you should be feeling better within the week."

After she leaves, I sing for a while but my voice is dry and scratchy. Then I try to read, but my eyes, both of them, keep closing. Can't write another letter to Bren since she didn't write back to me yet. Don't want to waste a whole day off school sleeping and scratching.

I dig around in my closet, looking for the needlepoint kit Nanny gave me for my birthday after I didn't exactly take to knitting like a house on fire. It's a picture of violets and daisies. Or it will be if I ever get it done.

My stomach starts growling before I finish one of the dark purple petals. I'm too dizzy to go downstairs, so I check my underwear drawer. Days-of-the-week panties, knee socks, leotards. No jawbreakers. No Popeye candy cigarettes. Not even any boring old peppermints.

I go back to my needlepoint, but having one eye closed makes me keep stabbing myself so I roll it up and stuff it inside my orange crate. Then I turn CKDH on low, listen to people selling tires and giving away kittens on "The Swap

Shop" and look at my books. I've read them all at least twice. Some of them, four times. If I knew I was gonna be sick, I would've gone to the library first.

I lie there for a while, just scratching and listening to the radio, until I hear Bethy crying. She starts off whimpering, like Skippy chasing rabbits in his sleep, but pretty soon she's screeching like a fire truck. Where's Mom?

I roll over and shut the radio off. Then I sit up real slow, to keep my head from spinning right off my shoulders into outer space. I swing my legs over the side of my bed, take a sip of water, then put on my slippers and drag my feet down the hall. Soon as I open her door, Bethy's howling gets ten times louder. The stink's worse than the outhouse at Heather Beach after Saturday night beans and wieners.

"What's wrong, Bethy? You poopy?" Her face looks like a smooshed red strawberry with a big wormhole in it. How could that tiny face have such an enormous mouth? I reach over the side of the crib to pick her up, but then I remember. *Chickenpox can be dangerous for little babies.* At least she slows down on the crying and tries to breathe when she sees me. I cover my ears to stop them from ringing and start singing.

"Puff the magic dragon, lived by the sea ..."

"No!"

I swallow my words and spin around. "Well, you don't need to holler."

"Sorry, Jenn. It's just I just don't want Bethy to catch

anything. She's still pretty little."

I stand in the doorway and watch Mom change Bethy's diaper.

"Hold still, Bethy. Stop being such a wiggle worm." Bethy smiles and makes that little bird cooing sound. Her tummy looks so pink and pudgy that Mom has to tickle her, just a little bit. Puts her lips on Bethy's belly and tries to blow raspberries, make her laugh, like Dad.

"How's mommy's little angel?"

Her big strong hands make doing the diaper pins look dead easy. "I'm sure glad you heard her, Jenn. You better get back to bed, though. Try to keep the germs in one place."

I turtle-walk back down the hall, scratching and wiggling. Mom's singing follows me. "Hush little baby, don't say a word; Mama's gonna buy you a mockingbird ..."

She used to sing to me, too.

When I was sick or had bad dreams.

When I was little. I'm not real sure what a mockingbird is, but I can say for certain she never bought me one.

CHAPTER 12

(WHEREIN Jenn Finds a Friend to Sing With)

Wednesday morning, I'm helping Mom organize the pickles and jam in the Ali Baba cave, which is really the little closet under the stairs, when Mom tells me we're having company.

"Melody's mom has to work, so I offered to look after her, since you both have the chickenpox," she says.

"She's got them, too?"

Mom nods and passes me a bottle of pink crabapple jelly. "She's had them for a few days. Think she was the first one in your class to get sick. Miss Creelman said most of the girls are home with it now."

"It must be real easy to catch," I say. "Wonder what she likes to play."

Melody's mom drops her off on her way to the prison.

She looks like Melody, only taller and with some long white hairs mixed in with the black ones. "Thank you so much, Margie," she says. "I hope she won't be any trouble for you."

"It's my pleasure, Pat," Mom says. "She'll keep Jennifer from going stir crazy." She gives me a smile-frown. "And driving *me* crazy!"

We watch baby shows on TV for a while, then Mom says we can use the hi-fi if we want. I pull the pocket doors closed so she can't hear us from the kitchen.

"You can have first pick." I get down on my knees, slide open the cabinet doors, and start flipping through the records.

Melody kneels down beside me. "Wow! I've never seen so many records. Do you have any Everly Brothers?"

"Never heard tell of them." I look through the big records again, and then the small ones in the paper sleeves. "All we have is this little 45. They look like Elvis." I snap the round plastic plug into the centre of it, then put it on the record player. I don't know the tune, so I sit on the couch and mumble the words to myself, same as I do in church. It's a mushy song about dreaming and wanting.

Partway through, I look at Melody. She's sitting in the big turquoise chair, mumbling at the floor, same as me, only she looks up when she feels me staring at her. We both laugh, then I lift the needle back to the start. We sing real quiet at first, both of us with our eyes glued to the stereo, but by the end, we're grinning and singing the chorus right out loud.

I never had a friend to sing with before. Miss Dill used to

ask Bren to mouth the words in choir. Bren and Wade.

"How do they do that?" I ask. "Make their two voices sound the same but different?"

"They're singing harmony. I was learning it at my old school. It's hard, but you have to listen for the second note above the melody—the melody's what the main singer's singing. Like this ... listen ..."

I listen as hard as I can while she sings the harmony part with one of the Everly Brothers. I try to hum along but it's real hard. "Neato," I say when she's done. "I forgot what it was called, but Miss Dill's all the time trying to get kids to sing harmony in the choir at school. Wish I could. I'm still trying to sing over my bridge—that's what Miss Dill calls high singing, moving from your low chest voice up to your high head voice."

I move the needle back to the start and try singing the harmony with her, but my voice keeps falling back down to the melody.

"You have to really know the scales, frontwards and backwards," she says. "C ... D ... E ... F ... G ... A ... B ... C. Then, if the main singer is on 'C,' you have to be on 'E.'"

"Maybe Miss Dill can help me. Did you used to have concerts at your old school?"

Melody shakes her head. "No. It wasn't a very good school. Some of the teachers there were mean, didn't like kids much. The ones here are all so nice."

"Where did you live before again?" I ask.

"Shubenacadie."

"That's a funny word."

"It's a Micmac word. Means place with lots of nuts. Maybe because there's lots of horse chestnut trees there."

"I think my Nanny used to work at that school. She wasn't a teacher, though, and it was a long time ago."

"My mom and dad both went to the same school. Maybe she knew them."

"Maybe." From the way Nanny talked about the Indian kids, I kind of hope she didn't. I get up to move the needle back. "Let's sing it again."

After the fifth time through, Mom slides the doors open just enough to poke her head in between. "Sorry to interrupt your fun, girls, but is that the only song we have? It's time for Bethy's nap now, anyway."

We laugh. "Want us to sing her to sleep?" I ask.

"Sure. I don't think you're contagious anymore, and I need to finish my baking for the church group bake sale. Eva's coming to pick up my lemon loaves later on."

I take Bethy from Mom, and we go upstairs.

"She's so sweet," Melody says. "I love babies. Can I hold her?"

"Let me check her diaper first. She won't settle if she's wet."

I lay Bethy down on the change table and unsnap her fuzzy yellow sleeper. "Hey, Bethy. Who's a pretty baby?" I rub noses with her, then roll her over, hold my breath, and peek inside her diaper. "Clean bum. She can be a little squirmy, but she loves to be rocked."

Melody sits down in the rocking chair, and I sit Bethy on her lap.

"Do you have any brothers or sisters?"

She starts to nod, then turns it into a headshake and smiles down at Bethy. "Does she have a favorite lullaby?"

"Usually I sing 'Puff' to her," I say. "And pat her back, just in case she needs one more burp."

"'Puff'? Was that the one you were singing in the library that day? I don't know it." Melody puts her cheek up against Bethy's. "She smells so good. Like spring."

"I'll teach you." I sit down on the braided rug beside them. "Puff, the magic dragon, lived by the sea, and frolicked in the autumn mist in a land called Honah Lee ..."

Bethy starts cooing straight away.

Melody smiles. "She sounds like a mourning dove."

I stop singing. "What's that—a bird that's only out in the mornings?"

She shakes her head. "I haven't seen them around here, but we had them around Shubie. They're real pretty. But it's mourning—like feeling sad, not the morning part of the day. They're a symbol of hope and peace. Some people say they carry people up to heaven."

"Really? We mostly have robins and pigeons around here," I say. "Don't know what they're a symbol of—poop, maybe." We giggle, then I go back to singing. Before I get to the verse about kings and princes and pirates, Bethy's eyelashes are fluttering. Melody gets up slowly, steps up on the stool and lays her down gently in the crib. We tiptoe out and down the hallway to my room.

"I like that song," Melody says.

"It gets a little sad near the end," I tell her. "About dragons living forever but not little boys. We've got the record. What do you want to do now?"

She sits down on my bed, looks around my room, and shrugs.

I pick up Cheeky and look across his fuzzy head at Melody. "Sometimes I still like to play house," I say, rubbing his rubber ears. "Even though it's a baby game."

She smiles. "I love playing house. You can be the mom."

Takes us about fifty trips to lug all my stuff down from the attic and out onto the front porch. My play dishes, Mom's old doll carriage and little wooden table and chairs, and Nanny's antique dress-up clothes. Melody's stuffing her ponytail up under Grampy's old fedora, and I'm helping Skippy with his people walking, when the Saunders' robin's-egg-blue station-wagon pokes its big nose into our driveway.

I push Skippy's paws up off my shoulders; he thumps back down to the floor and woofs.

"Don't let on we were playing house." I yank the tennis balls out from under my sweater and wipe my Mandarin Orange lipstick off on my sleeve.

Melody rips Bethy's pink baby bonnet off Skippy and spits on her hand to try and rub off her tea-leaf moustache.

Sarah gets out and slams the car door. Her Royal Lowness

gets out the other side and follows her up the walkway. "Now, don't take off your church gloves, Sarah Jane. You don't want to scar your beautiful skin." You can hardly see her face for the smoke, but Mrs. Saunders' Queen voice is loud and clear.

Melody keeps her head down and packs up the dishes.

Sarah bounces up the steps in her shiny black boots. "Hey, Blinky—were you just slow-dancing with that mutt?"

Her gray eyes zip around the porch like the silver pin balls in "Humpty Dumpty" at the bowling alley. Then she snorts and hee-haws. "You're not playing house!"

None of your beeswax, I want to say. Instead, I say, "I was babysitting the neighbor's kids last week."

She stares at my forehead. "Looks like you've got a third eye, that one on your head's so big."

I blush and brush my bangs back over it. "I know."

"Hello, Jennifer." Mrs. Saunders stops at the bottom of the steps. Grinds her cigarette out with the toe of one red high heel shoe, then digs a little mirror out of her purse, flips it open, and smears on more lipstick. Fire Engine Red. Mom saves that color for Saturday night dances at the fire hall.

Skippy trots over. Gets down on his elbows, then shoves his bum up in the air and barks.

Her Royal Lowness backs up. "For heaven's sake—keep that creature away from me."

I grab Skippy by the collar. "Bad dog, Skippy!"

Mrs. Saunders snaps her purse shut, then walks up the

stairs on her toes, so her heels don't get stuck between the boards. Pulls her white sunglasses down to the end of her nose and sniffs, like Skippy just pooped. "And who is this ... child?"

"Melody," I say. "Melody Syliboy. She's new."

"I see." Her Royal Lowness looks at Melody's black rubber boots; slowly moves her eyes up past Melody's green jumper to her hair, then finally her face. "I believe I met your mother at the church sale a few months ago."

Melody nods at the toes of her boots.

"Isn't it lovely that she's found some employment, working for my husband up at the prison?" She puts both hands up to her beehive hairdo, gives Melody a smirkle.

Melody nods again, then Mrs. Saunders turns and pulls open the screen door. "Yoo hoo! Margie! I'm here for your goodies."

Sarah flips her hair back and stares across the porch at Melody. "What's wrong with your lip, Pocahontas? Is that dirt?"

"Nothin'. No." Melody blushes, then covers what's left of her mustache with her fingers. "It's just chickenpox."

Sarah turns around so her back's facing Melody. "Did you hear My Mother's getting Annie Murray to give me singing lessons, Blinky? Private vocal lessons?"

I shake my head. "You're lucky. Annie used to keep house for us."

"She did?" Sarah looks disappointed, then she tosses her hair back. "Oh, you mean back before she got famous."

"Uh-huh. When I was little."

"All set, sweetheart?" The screen door bangs shut behind Mrs. Saunders.

"Yes, Mother." Sarah looks back at me. "See you at school, Jennifer."

"Bye." I stand beside Melody as they walk back to their car. Act like I'm not watching and listening, only I am.

"You kept your distance, did you, darling?" Mrs. Saunders whispers. Only it's the loudest whisper I ever heard.

"Of course. She already gave everybody the chickenpox."

Her mother pats Sarah's arm. "That's my girl. Straighten up, sweetie pie. You're slouching again."

I can almost hear Sarah's shiny boot heels clicking together as she pushes her shoulders back and marches down the driveway.

The car doors slam shut and they back out onto the street. I squint my eyes up and try to put a hex on them so they'll back into a telephone pole, but they don't.

"Sarah's spoiled rotten," I say. "Like Veronica in the Archie comics, only with blonde hair like Betty. Her dad's one of the bosses up at the new prison. My dad's just a bookkeeper."

"She's so lucky." Melody sits down on the top step beside me. "Wish we had a big fancy car like that. And that I had blonde hair and blue eyes."

"Why?"

"It's just easier. People are nicer to you when you don't have brown skin. There are lots of good things about being Native, but mostly I wish I wasn't."

I look at her. "Because kids are mean to you?"

She nods. "I'm the only one at school with brown skin."

"There's the Clykes and the Ruddicks," I say. "Only they're not in our class."

"And they're colored people. Negroes. Their skin's black."

"They call it black, but it's really chocolate brown. Do you know Mr. Ruddick, the singing miner?"

She shakes her head.

"Well, after the Big Bump, some of the miners got invited to have a holiday in the State of Georgia in the u.s. of a. When the boss of Georgia found out Mr. Ruddick was a colored man, he made Mr. Ruddick have his holiday in a whole different place from the white miners, away from his friends."

Melody frowns and sits down on one of the little chairs. "But that's not fair. It's so mean."

"Yup. And Mr. Ruddick's a real nice man." I rub my cheeks with both hands. "Wish I had skin like yours. It's like the sand at Heather Beach," I say. "Or taffy. And you don't have any ugly freckles. In the summer, I'm just one big freckle."

She laughs. "It's easier, having white skin. Even if you're mean, like Junior and Sarah, people still think you're good."

"That doesn't even make sense." I sit down across from her and pretend I'm pouring tea from the blue and white plastic teapot into the little cups. "You're a hundred times nicer than them."

"Mmm ... The Elders say our ancestors lived here ages before the white man came."

"But there are heaps more white people now. How did that happen?"

Melody shrugs, then leans forward, rests her elbows on her knees, folds her hands in front of her. "My people got pushed off their land, crowded onto the Reservations, instead of living with nature like before. White people took over."

I stare at her. "But that's terrible. It's like stealing. Did the white people have to go to prison?"

Melody shakes her head. "Don't think so. Maybe they didn't have prisons way back then. And the white man brought guns with him. It'd be hard for arrows to argue with bullets."

"Did your dad know how to hunt with a bow and arrow?"

Melody takes a sip of pretend tea and nods. "He was going to teach me, me and my br- ..." She sucks in some air, sets down her cup, and stops talking.

"Sarah's like a hunter, only with words instead of arrows. She picks on people for all sorts of reasons, not just their skin. Like my bad eye, and Vickie's chubby belly."

"But, why?" Melody asks.

I shrug. "She's just mean. And she thinks she's such a great singer. Skippy sings better than her. Annie Murray could give her a hundred lessons and she'd still sound like a crow with laryngitis."

Melody giggles. "Why does she call you Blinky?"

"See my scar? Junior binged me with a rock last year. My eye still works, but when I'm sick or bothered, it slams shut.

Gets me in a pickle when people think I'm giving them the wink."

"Does it hurt?"

"Not anymore." I rub the scar with my pointer finger. "But I had to wear a patch for six weeks last year. Long Jenn Silver. What do you want to do now?"

She shrugs. "We could listen to the radio."

"Okay. We can clean this stuff up later. Let's go up to my room."

I sit cross-legged on my bed and she sits in my little rocking chair. The one that used to be Dad's.

"That's a real nice transistor," Melody says. "It's so small. How does it work?"

I show her how to turn it on.

After the news, the announcer says the name of the next song. I sit up straight and pop my eyes open at Melody. "*What* did he say? Springhill! Our Springhill?"

We sit still and listen all the way through.

"In the town of Springhill, you don't sleep easy. Often the earth will tremble and groan ..."

"Peter, Paul, and Mary," I say, when it's done. "The same singers as 'Puff'!"

"They're real good at singing harmony," Melody says. "But it's such a sad song."

I nod. "I think it's about The Big Bump."

"What's that—like a mountain?"

I shake my head. "Sort of an earthquake down in the mines. Lots of men got squished between the floor and the tunnel roof. Same year I was born—1958. My Grampy died, but my Uncle Charlie got rescued after twelve days underground. He didn't get to be on the Ed Sullivan show, though. I think they only picked the good singers, like Mr. Ruddick."

Melody smiles. "What kind of mine? Diamonds? Like in *Snow White and the Seven Dwarfs*?"

"Nope. Coal. Stinky black coal. The mines are all closed up now, except for one, but sometimes sinkholes still show up in people's backyards. If you aren't careful, you can fall right down into a tunnel," I tell her. "Like Alice in Wonderland in the rabbit hole."

"I'll be real careful, then." Melody shivers. "I don't much like the dark."

"We still have small bumps sometimes," I say. "The earth still trembles and groans, like in the song. Dad says it's just the coal reminding us it's still down there."

"I've felt them a few times," she says. "I thought they were earthquakes."

"Well, they are, sort of. Bet somebody will sing that at the Miners' Hall Concert," I say. "I'm gonna ask Miss Dill if she's got the music."

CHAPTER 13

(WHEREIN Jenn Meets Jimmy)

"Why do these nasty chickens have so many babies?" I dig at a big one underneath my bangs.

"Feels like I'm gonna scratch the skin right off my belly," Melody says. "If we were snakes, we could get a whole new set of skin."

"Really?"

She nods. "Haven't you ever seen an empty snakeskin in the grass?"

"Nope, but I'd like to. Especially an empty one—I'm scared of snakes. Lucky your mom had to work again today," I say. "So we could scratch together."

Melody nods. "I'm pretty sure I've got more than you, though."

"Whoever invented chickenpox must have been one mean, nasty son-of-a-gun," I say. "Somebody like Wade."

"Only he'd never be smart enough to invent anything."

Mom brings us up toasted peanut butter and banana sandwiches for lunch. "It's the oddest thing. I went out to the garden to dig up some carrots for supper, and a bunch had already been pulled. A fat ripe tomato I had my eye on is gone, too."

"Did they ever find the escaped prisoner?" I ask.

She shrugs. "Haven't heard anything about that for weeks. When you come downstairs, I'll show you the clever birdfeeder the thief left in the maple tree by the shed. It's just adorable—made of birchbark and twigs." She stares at my forehead. "Have you been picking at that big one?"

I squirm. "I can't help it. The scab's soooo... itchy."

Mom goes back downstairs, then brings us up some white Sunday school gloves. "So your pox won't get infected."

"Maybe we should always wear gloves," Melody says after she leaves. "So we don't catch more germs, real germs, I mean."

"Yeah. Maybe I'd stop biting my nails then, too."

"It'd be hard to write with gloves on, though, especially practicing penmanship." Melody tries writing her name on my shoebox full of crayons and colored pencils. "Feels like I've got five thumbs."

"I bet the Queen of England can write with gloves on," I say. "She probably never takes hers off. Well, maybe to use the bathroom."

"Does the Queen even use the toilet? What would she do with her purse?" Just thinking about that makes us laugh our heads off for about ten minutes.

"Wonder if Sarah and Penny and them still have the chickenpox?"

Melody shrugs.

"Serves them right," I say. "MSG and all that."

"Hmmm ... only, what did we do to deserve the chickenpox?"

"Absolutely nothing," I say. "We're perfect angels." I turn the radio on. "Oh, I love this one. It's The Turtles—'So Happy Together.'"

Melody picks up my big silver brush off the dresser. Holds it up to her lips and sings with me.

"Wonder why all the bands have animal names?" I say. "Monkees, Turtles ..."

She giggles. "Yeah. *Buck* Owens, *Buffalo* Springfield ..."

"The Miners' Hall concert's really fun," I say. "Maybe we could sing a duet."

Melody shakes her head. "I could never. All those strangers ..."

"Let's talk to Miss Dill when we get back to school. Maybe we could wear a disguise. Dress up like miners. Or Draegermen."

"What are Draegermen?"

"Rescue miners. They wear these gas masks that make them look like Martians. My Uncle Charlie used to be a Draegerman. His mask's still hanging in Nanny's barn."

"It might be hard to sing with a gas mask on," Melody says.

"Hmmm ... I'm still gonna ask Miss Dill if she's got the music for that Springhill song. Just in case," I say.

After lunch, Mom says we can go for a bike ride. "Just around the neighborhood," she says. "After all, it is a school day, and you're still officially 'sick.' Bethy and I are just going up for a short nap."

We get my bike out, then ride double around the block.

"Can I show you something?" Melody says.

"Where?"

"Out by the prison. It's not far."

I look back at my house. "Okay, but we need to be fast." Partway up Wakeup Hill, by the prison field, we have to get off and walk. I take a big sniff. "Mmmm... Somebody just cut their hay." There's a few prisoners out working in the stubbly field. One of them's singing "Are you Lonesome Tonight?" When he sees us, he stops digging. Stands still and stares. It's the same Elvis one.

I look down at my bike. "He's a good singer," I say. "He doesn't even look scary."

"Mmmm ..." Even though I was the one doing the pedaling, Melody's face is all red. We get back on and coast down the other side. Just before Nanny's lane, Melody says, "Turn here." I turn up a skinny dirt path I never noticed before. Through a dried-up cornfield.

"Hope Nanny doesn't see us," I say. "Where are we going?"

Melody points over my shoulder into the woods. "You'll see."

After the cornfield, when the grass gets too long, we get off and I lean my bike up against a pine tree. With one of Nanny's *No Trespassing* signs on it. "There's a cave out here," I say.

Melody nods. "I know."

"How'd you know about it? I never brought you out to Nanny's."

"Can you keep a secret?"

"I'm the best secret keeper. You could ask Bren—only she's not here." I stand up and make an x on my chest. "Cross my heart and hope to ... well, not really."

She stops walking, closes her eyes and lifts her face up to the fluffy clouds floating across the blue sky. Presses her thumbs together and puts them up to her mouth. Like she's making a grass whistle. Or praying. She folds her hands together, puffs up her cheeks, wiggles the fingers on one hand up and down, and blows between her thumb knuckles. It makes a hooting sound, like a wobbly owl laugh.

I shiver and rub my arms. "That's spooky. Gives me the heebie jeebies."

"Shhh!" Melody holds up one hand. "Listen."

I stare into the trees and hold my breath. Another loon yodel, a louder one, floats out over the pointy tops of the pine trees. It's shaky and eerie, like a real loon. But peaceful, too.

Melody puts her hands up again and answers. A few seconds later, another call comes, like an echo on the breeze. She pushes the hair back from her face and smiles. "Jimmy showed me. When I was only four. It's our safe call."

"Who's Jimmy?" I ask. "And will you teach me to do that?"

Before she can answer, I see a flash of somebody sprinting through the Christmas trees. I duck behind Melody. It's somebody with long hair, almost as long as hers, only it runs like a boy. He's got a red bandana wrapped around his head and he's wearing a barn jacket. Grampy's gray plaid barn jacket. And overalls like Nanny's, with barn rope tied around his waist. And a big knife hanging off it.

Melody hugs the boy, then turns to me. "Jimmy, this is my new friend, Jennifer."

He reaches out to shake my hand but I shove mine, both of them, inside their Sunday school gloves, deep into my pockets. He looks wild, like the Indians in the cowboy movies.

"Why does he have that big knife?" I ask.

"I'm a hunter. I use it to get food," Jimmy says. "That's all." He's not very big but his voice is really deep, like a man.

"Does he live in the woods?" I ask Melody. "Like the Indians on TV?"

Jimmy laughs and crosses his arms in front of his chest like Tonto. "Yes, Kemosabe. Me live in teepee."

I turn away when I feel my face getting red.

Melody smiles, then puts a finger to her lips. "Don't tell anybody. About my brother, I mean."

"He's your *brother*!" I frown and rub my hot ears. "Thought you said you didn't have a brother. And why is he a secret?"

"Nobody's supposed to know he's here." She squeezes my arm. "Promise me you won't tell?"

I nod and draw another x on my chest, then look back at Jimmy. He looks like Melody's twin. Only with a different birthday. Is he the escaped prisoner?

We follow him down the path to Nanny's coal cave. There's a neat pile of firewood next to a circle of black stones. A red kerosene lantern's standing on a stump.

"You're the mystery thief!" I say. "The one that's been leaving the presents."

He frowns. "No! Well ... I'm not a thief, but I do need to borrow things. I try to pay people back by making them things, or leaving them gifts."

"Why are you camping out here?" I ask. "Is it like a game?"

He snort laughs. "It's not exactly camping. Not for fun. I'm hungry a lot, and it's getting cold at nights."

"I try to bring him some food," Melody says. "But it's hard for me to get out here sometimes."

"Can we look inside the cave?" I ask. "With the lantern?"

Before he can answer, Nanny's old truck rumbles and rattles down the lane, off in the distance. "We've gotta go," I say. "If Nanny catches us, she'll have a million questions about what we're doing out here, and Mom'll kill me for leaving the neighborhood."

Melody hugs Jimmy, then we race back to my bike. When we get to the rows of cornstalks, we hop on and I start pedaling between them, back out to Black River Road.

"Doesn't Jimmy go to school?" I ask.

"That's how come he's a secret. Why he's hiding out in the woods. Because he ran away from his school. The School for Boys. It's a horrible place with devils for teachers."

"Why? Why can't he just live with you and your mom? Go to regular school."

"He's almost eighteen; his birthday's soon. Then he'll be an adult and they can't make him go back to that school. They treat the boys like slaves. You can't tell anybody else." She squeezes me hard around my middle. "Not even your parents."

"I won't! I promise." I pedal hard for a few minutes. "Does your mom know he's here?"

She goes stiff behind me. "No! I mean, you can't tell her. If she knew, she'd get in big trouble with the police. They already came looking for him a few times. Trying to take him back to the school."

"Hey, was it Jimmy at the Pit Pond that day?"

"Uh-huh. I was taking him some food when we saw you fall in."

"I knew it! I should've told him thank you." I stop pedaling and put my feet down. "I'm out of breath. We need to walk, just to the top of the hill."

When we get to the top, we get on again and coast back to town. We don't talk much. I've got lots of questions, but it doesn't seem like Melody wants to talk about Jimmy. It's like a Hardy Boys mystery, only with a real kid. Why did

Jimmy have to go to that horrible school? And why can't his mother help him? What will he do when the snow comes? Or if Nanny and her shotgun find him? Or even worse, the police ...

After Melody's mom picks her up, I wander into the kitchen. Bethy's sitting in the middle of the table in her yellow ducky chair. Dad's stuffing some white mush into her and pretending to gobble up her pink jellybean toes at the same time.

He winks at me. "Carnation milk and rice cereal—want some? Used to be your favorite. Back when you were my little Butterball, instead of a Skinny Minny."

I give him a yuck face, pull my chair out, and sit down at the table.

"How are you, Jenny?" Mom's eyebrows pop up into a tent shape, and her eyes go all watery. Do I look that bad?

I get up and look at myself in the old wavy mirror by the back door. Push all my hair back so I can get a real good look. Then I shake my head and groan. "I look like a giant connect-the-pimples picture. They're even on my lips." I tilt my head back. "And up my nose! That's so gross." I wiggle my whole body. "And I'm itchy, really itchy. Wish I was a snake so I could just get a whole new set of skin."

Mom picks Beth up from her chair and gives her an Eskimo kiss. She giggles and itches her nose with her sticky fingers.

"Hope Bethy doesn't get the chickenpox," I say.

"Mmmm ... Mommy's itty bitty angel's too little to scratch for herself." Mom's smiling, but it's the kind of smile you have to squeeze out of a frown.

I watch Bugs Bunny for a while, then go back upstairs. Art Linkletter and the kids are on the radio. A little boy with a helium-balloon voice is crying about the tooth monster stealing all his teeth.

Dad knocks, then comes in and sits on the edge of my bed. "You should be on the radio with Art. You could sing."

"Maybe ... if we move to California, or New York City, or wherever they are."

He sticks out his hand. "Slap my hand and we'll go wherever you want for our holidays next summer."

I groan. "D-a-a-a-d! You always pull it away when I pick someplace good."

He grins. "You never know. Come on. Try me."

"All right. P.E.I.!" I shout, then try to slap his hand.

He yanks it away too fast.

"New York City!" I shout. I stare into his eyes, hold my hand up, do a couple of fakes, then slap his hand. A full one!

"No fair," he says. "You faked me out."

"You promised. We can meet Ed Sullivan!"

He grins and holds up the fingers on his other hand. They're crossed. "New York City's an awful big place. But we'll see ... Sweet dreams, Jenny."

"No fair! You promised!"

After Dad leaves, I snuggle up to Cheeky and push my

face into the cool side of my pillow. Wish I could tell Mom and Dad about Jimmy. Maybe they could help him. Tell the police not to send him back to that devil school. Tell them to take Wade and Junior instead.

When my pillow gets warm, I flip it over. Back and forth; back and forth. Why won't the big oozy pock in the middle of my forehead stop itching? I give up and pull one glove off, just for a minute, so I can give it one good long scratch before I fall asleep. Feels so great I don't even worry about the third eye I'm probably gonna have for the whole entire rest of my life.

Mom looks funny when she comes to tuck me in: squinty, like somebody's playing a drum solo inside her head.

"Mrs. MacLellan's downstairs." Her mouth is smiling, but her eyes look like she's in outer space. "She's going to sit with you for a while—Bethy's running a bit of a fever so we're just going to pop up to All Saints to see Doc Murray."

I forget about scratching and sit up straight. "Can I come?"

She shakes his head. "I'm sure it's nothing, but I just want Dr. Murray to make sure everything's hunky-dory."

I pull off one of my gloves and start chewing on my fingernails. My eye twitches. Mostly the doctor comes here when I'm sick. Bethy must be really sick.

"Why doesn't he just come here to see Bethy?" I ask.

"He's tied up helping somebody deliver a baby at the hospital," Mom says. "We won't be long. Mrs. MacLellan's downstairs if you need anything." She leans over and kisses my forehead.

"Good job you missed my third eye. Goodnight, Mom."

"Goodnight, Jenny."

"Can you ask Dr. Murray if Annie could come sing at my next birthday party? If she's not too busy singing on television?"

Mom laughs. "I'll see what I can do, Jenny, but I expect Annie's pretty busy with the folks on *Singalong Jubilee.*"

"Does that make us famous, too, because she used to keep house for us?" I ask.

"It's possible," she says. "Did you get her to autograph anything for you?"

"No, but I have that picture of Sir Skips A Lot she drew for me."

"Better hang on to that," she says. "In case she gets really famous and starts making her own records."

"Could that *really* happen to somebody from Springhill?"

"Anything's possible. All famous people had to grow up someplace."

"Probably that'll happen to me, then. After I save up enough money to take singing lessons," I say. "And get over my fainting."

"You sing like an angel," Mom says. "Even without lessons. Maybe you'll have your own singing group someday. You and Bethy and Melody. Dad could play the guitar for you."

"Mmmm ... maybe. Give Bethy a smoochy kiss for me."

After she turns out the light and closes the door, my watch

ticking and the wind ghost whistling down the chimney are the only sounds left.

When the wind picks up, the pine-branch needle fingers scratching on my window give me the willies, same as Miss Creelman's pointy fingernails on the blackboard. I shiver, then turn on my lamp and get out my ladybug paper.

Dear Bren:

I'm sorry I didn't write to you lately but I've got the chickenpox so I've been busy scratching—with Melody. She's a real good singer and there's a new song about the Big Bump that we might sing for the Miners' Hall Concert. I have a big secret but I'm not allowed to tell.

Mom and Dad just took Bethy to the hospital. I hope she's not getting the chickenpox. I'm sleepy but I'll write more tomorrow. I guess you must be busy too since I didn't get any letters from you in a long, long time.

Jenn

After I'm done writing, I practice my scales five times; I almost make it up to high F the last time, but then my voice cracks in the middle of my bridge. I turn off my lamp and listen for Old Red in the driveway. I'm still listening when the ten o'clock church chimes ring.

CHAPTER 14

(WHEREIN Melody Comes for a Sleepover)

Before I open my eyes in the morning, I know Nanny's in the room. Even when she's not at home, she smells like moth balls and her critters.

"Good morning, Jennifer Elizabeth." Nanny rolls up the blind, turns around, and pulls her round granny glasses down to the end of her nose and looks over top of them at me. Her eyes are the color of ripe blueberries. "Time to haul your carcass out of bed. I brought you a little something."

I reach out, take the paper bag from her, and pull the handles apart. I'm sorry it's not some of her mushy Harlequin romances that she hides in her bathroom closet, but I smile anyway. "Dad's little blue books! *Reddy Fox, Jimmy Skunk, Buster Bear, Old Mother West Wind ...*"

"I know you already read them all, but you can read them

to the baby," Nanny says. "When she's a bit bigger."

"And chicken bones! But it's not even Christmas. Can we have one now, Nanny?" I put my hands up and beg like Skippy. "Pretty please, with peanut butter fudge frosting on top?"

"Best cure for whatever ails you." She snorts. "Your mother and me don't see eye to eye on that, but a bit of candy never did a body any harm."

"How come you're here so early?" It's hard to talk and suck on a chicken bone at the same time, but the pink pepperminty part makes me smile before I even get to the yummy melty chocolate hiding inside. I've got the butterfly belly feeling that I'm supposed to be worrying about something, but I can't think what it is.

I crunch into my chicken bone then sit up real quick. "Where's Mom?" My heart starts thumping like Skippy scratching his armpit with the sharp toenails on his back feet. "And Bethy?" I bite the side of my tongue. My salty blood all mixed up with chocolaty peppermint and worry makes my belly woozy.

I push back my cozy quilt and stand up. "Are they home?"

"Still in bed. They were late getting home from the hospital last night."

I blink, pick Cheeky up, and press my cheek up against his fuzzy head. Is Bethy going to die? Like Melody's dad? What would Nanny say if I asked her? *Lord have mercy, Jennifer! I certainly hope not. She only just got done being born.*

I poke my finger in between my buttonholes, scratch my

growling belly, and stare hard at Nanny. She stares straight back at me without even blinking, like an owl.

"I'm hungry," I say. "Can I eat before they get up?"

"I expect I could rustle you up some flapjacks," Nanny says. "Brought a jug of maple syrup, tapped by yours truly."

"Yummy!"

"I'll be downstairs—you hustle yourself into some clothes. No lollygagging!"

While I'm eating, Nanny sits down beside me in Dad's chair. "Your mother says that Indian girl's coming over for supper. Staying the night."

I sit up straight and grin. "She is?"

"I'm sticking around to give your mother a hand. You'd best not get up to any trouble when I'm in charge." Nanny shakes her finger at me. "No whooping and craziness. You hear? And no peeing the bed. Be sure and tell her that."

I nod.

When Melody shows up at suppertime, she's wearing a party dress under her brown striped sweater. A poofy yellow party dress. The exact same poofy dress Sarah had for her eighth birthday party.

"I like your dress," I say. "It's like Elnora's fancy graduation dress."

Her face turns pink. "Mom bought it for me. I don't really like it, but I wore it so she wouldn't feel bad. I like your slacks."

I look down at my new striped bellbottoms. "Yeah. Wish

I could wear them to school instead of dresses and skirts all the time. This is my first sleepover since Bren left."

She smiles. "It's my first sleepover, too."

"Ever?"

She nods.

"Geez. Bren and me used to have sleepovers every month. Every week in the summer."

We're just settling in to watch Ed Sullivan, when the Saunders' car turns into the driveway. "Must be Eva returning my pans," Mom says. "If she brings Sarah, make sure to include her, Jenn."

I roll my eyes at Melody. While Mom's answering the doorbell, I grab Melody by the sleeve and pull her into the kitchen. Put my mouth right up next to her ear. "The Ali Baba cave. Quick, in here ..."

I turn the brown knob on the little wood door under the stairs real slow so it doesn't squeak. The jars of pickles and jam inside sparkle like emeralds and rubies and gold when the light hits them. "Buried treasure!" I whisper.

Melody giggles, only she looks kind of nervous. I close the door behind us and go easy on the knob so it doesn't click. Soon as the light disappears, Melody grabs on to my arm.

I look at her but I can't see her even with her crouching right next to me. She's breathing funny, like she just ran a race.

"Shhhh ..."

"Is Jennifer home?" Sarah asks.

"She's here somewhere," Mom says. "Why don't you look in her room?"

Sarah thuds up the stairs right on top of us.

"She better not stick her rat nose into my stuff," I whisper.

"This stealing has gotten completely out of hand." Mrs. Saunders' heels click past the closet door on her way to the kitchen. "Mr. Alick's kerosene lantern vanished from his back porch. Art supplies stolen from the church. Seems the police are just twiddling their thumbs—either that or taking a few too many doughnut breaks."

"Did you hear if that escaped prisoner was ever found?" Mom asks.

"I don't know about that," Her Royal Lowness says. Then she makes her voice low, but it's a real loud whisper. "Just between you, me, and the gatepost, I have my suspicions. Sarah Jane said the Indian girl's been taking things from her at school. Two brand-new velvet headbands just last week and a sweater the week before that. I'm quite certain it was her gave all the girls the chickenpox."

The white part of Melody's brown eyes looks spooky, and she's humming. Her breath's all hot chocolate and Nanny's macaroni goulash. "Shhh!" I say.

She squeezes my wrist even tighter, like she's trying to give me an Indian Burn, but she doesn't say anything, just keeps humming.

"Jennifer's cousins in Halifax had the chickenpox not long ago. I assume that's where she picked them up. Melody seems like a perfectly nice little girl to me," Mom says.

"She's been spending some time with Jenn while they're recuperating from the chickenpox."

"Oh, my," Mrs. Saunders says. "Do you think that's a good idea, Margie? We are judged by the company we keep, after all."

"Well, you know what they say. Innocent until proven guilty." Mom's using her mad voice and slamming the cupboard doors shut.

I try to pull my arm away from Melody's squeezing but she won't let go. "You're pinching me," I whisper. I have to hunch my shoulder up to hide my ear from her tickly breath. Then she starts making this creepy low moaning sound, like Skippy when it thunders. Starts muttering in some weird language, like the priest at the Catholic Church.

Why would Melody know priest talk?

"Hush up!" My eyes feel as if they're big and thirsty now, sucking up all the tiny bits of light there are. Melody's are closed up tight. "Is that mumbo-jumbo Pig-Latin? I used to know it but I forget. Will you teach me?"

Mom and Mrs. Saunders walk past the closet to the front door. "Now, I really must get back to the baby. She hasn't been feeling well," Mom says. "Thank you for returning my pans."

"Sarah Jane, my pet, we're ready to go now," Mrs. Saunders calls up the stairs. "You can play with Jennifer another time."

Sarah pounds down the stairs.

"Maybe Jenn's up in the attic. I'll just come out with

you, roll up the windows in the car," Mom says. "Looks like it might rain." The screen door squeaks open, then snaps shut.

Melody starts shivering, even though it's so hot in the closet you can't hardly breathe. And she's got on her sweater. Her earthquake shaking makes the jam jars clink against each other on the shelves behind us. Like Nanny's old windows when there's a bump. My hand's all pins and needles from Melody grabbing onto it like a climbing rope.

"What are you doing, Sarah?" Her Royal Lowness shouts. "We have to go."

The screen door creaks open again. "Forgot my sweater," Sarah yells. Then she hisses, "I know you're in here, Blinky. I can smell Silly Boy."

The empty bottles on the top shelf start tinkling together. The floor starts vibrating and the door rattles. Melody's mumbling gets louder.

"I think it's a bump—just a little one," I whisper. When I put my hand over Melody's mouth, my funny bone hits one of the shelves. A pickle jar jiggles off it and thumps me in the side. Before I can twist around and catch it, it smashes onto the floor.

"Ahhhh!" My stomach starts flipping somersaults from the stink of sauerkraut, and my throat's full of a throw-up burp. I plug my nose and go to stand up. Only my shoulder hits underneath the bottom shelf.

Canning jars and juice bottles crash into each other like glass dominoes. They jump off the shelves and bang into us, smash onto the floor and explode into a gazillion pieces.

On top of all that commotion, Melody stops moaning and starts screeching. Like she's being murdered in cold blood.

.

CHAPTER 15

(WHEREIN Melody Tells Her Story)

Dad yanks the door open and we burst out, holding on to each other and squinting like moles. I fall into him and start laughing. Then, all of a sudden, I'm crying at the same time and trying to breathe.

Gooey pink blobs of rhubarb jam and disgusting stringy cabbage stick to my bell bottoms and blue sweater. Melody's yellow dress has got purple beet juice all over. Her hand, the one not glued to my arm, is bleeding. My bad eye droops shut and my head's full of feathers, like I'm gonna float away, or faint, like at the Music Festival.

Melody's done screaming. She doesn't say anything. Just stands there staring at the stinky mess splattered all over the floor, like animal guts on the highway.

"Holy Cow! Are you girls all right?" Dad lifts Melody's arm

up over her head, then grabs onto one of my shoulders and stares at my eyes, like they can talk.

I wipe my eyes on a clean part of my sleeve and nod at Dad. Mom, Her Royal Lowness, and the Queen Smirkle Bee are right behind him.

The porch door slams and Nanny comes in from the garden with a basket of potatoes. "What in tarnation's all the screeching about?" She stops, stares at the mess, then frowns at Melody.

Melody's Bambi eyes look like she's gone someplace else. Someplace safe.

"It was just a little bump. The coal reminding us it's still there. Let's get you up to the bathroom." Dad swats Skippy's rear to shoo him away, then he closes the closet door. "No, Skippy. Git!" He pulls back Melody's sleeve and holds up her bleeding arm as he leads us upstairs.

"Just a little accident," Mom says. "Thank you again for returning my pans, Eva."

"But what on earth happened? I've never heard such a commotion."

"We'll look after it," Mom says firmly. "Good night." The front door clicks closed behind Sarah and Her Mother.

"Good thing you girls had thick sweaters on," Dad says. Melody turns her head away and squeezes her eyes shut when Dad plucks the shiny piece of pickle jar out of the skin on her wrist. "It's a nice clean little piece. I'm sure I got all of it. The cut's not very deep—it just happened to hit a vein." He digs his hanky out of his pocket and ties it tight around

Melody's elbow. "This'll keep the blood from getting to your wrist, but keep your arm up over your head, too, sweetie; it'll stop bleeding soon enough."

I pick off some of the sauerkraut and jam globs and drop them into the toilet. Dad runs some steamy water in the sink and roots around in the medicine chest.

"You okay, Melody? It's all right—about the pickles and jam, I mean. Nanny's got heaps more bottles, hundreds probably. Maybe thousands. She could open up her own store, even." I close the toilet lid, step up onto it, and pull Melody's striped sleeve up off her bleeding arm.

Melody looks up at me and nods. "I'm scared of them," she whispers.

"Pickles and jam?" I whisper back. Dad's still busy looking in the medicine chest and whistling to make it seem like everything's hunky-dory.

"Closets." Melody's bottom lip wobbles, and her brown eyes look like giant tadpoles in the Pit Pond. She sniffs, then wipes her nose on the towel. "I'm sorry."

Dad cleans Melody's cut, then he makes an "I'm sorry" face and holds up the brown mercurochrome bottle. "It'll only sting for a second." Melody catches her breath and bites her lip when he dabs it on. He smears some Ozonol on the cut, covers it with a Band Aid, one of the big ones, then opens the door quietly. "I'll send Mom up in a few minutes."

When we get to my room, Melody gets her PJ's out of her grocery bag, then I sit in my little rocking chair, hum and face the closet while she puts them on.

"You can turn around, now," she says.

"Are you okay?" I ask.

Melody nods, then puts her empty bag on my dresser with a little brown pouch on top of it. Must be her toothbrush. Guess she didn't bring any extra clothes. Her PJ's have faded black kittens on them, and they're supposed to be long sleeves but they only get to her elbows. The bottoms are like pedal pushers. Her furry slippers flop around her skinny ankles.

"I've never seen slippers like that," I say.

She bends over, takes one off, and hands it to me. "They're moccasins. They were my mom's. My grandma made them for her from deerskin and rabbit fur."

"Real bunny fur? I love bunnies! They're so soft." I hold the gray fur up to my cheek, then run my fingers over the design. "And pretty. It must have taken a hundred years to sew on all those tiny beads."

Melody nods, then she looks out the window while I get into my pink daisy PJ's.

When somebody knocks "shave and a haircut" on my door, we both jump and giggle, then I shout out, *Two cents!*"

"Everybody decent? Can I come in?" Mom sticks her head around the door. "I brought you up some Kool-Aid and cookies." She sets the wooden tray down on my orange crate. Tries to cover up her worried face with a giant smile, like the guy on the Kool-Aid packages.

"You hungry?" I ask.

"No, thank you." Melody shakes her head. "Maybe later."

"Did we miss Ed Sullivan?" I get up and hand Mom our pile of dirty clothes. "And does pickle juice and blood come out?"

"Ed'll be on again next week." She pulls Melody's yellow dress out of the pile and looks it over. Shakes her head, then balloons up her cheeks and whooshes out a big bunch of air. "That's nothing the Laundry Fairy and a little club soda won't look after. It'd be a crying shame for such a pretty dress to get stained."

Mom sits down next to Melody, puts one hand on her shoulder and turns her wrist over to look at the Band Aid. Like she's checking Dad's work. "Are you okay, sweetie?" Her eyebrows make an upside-down v. "Can I do anything for you? Do you want to go home?"

Melody stares at the rug and shakes her head again."No, thank you, Mrs. Parsons," she whispers. "Mom's working. I'm sorry for the bother. I feel very tired, that's all."

"I'll give your mom a call later on, then. Just to let her know what happened. Do you want Jenn to keep you company?"

Melody nods. "I think my mom's off at seven."

"I'll come back up after I tuck Bethy in. She's coughing a lot—hope she'll be able to sleep." Mom starts to close the door, then sticks her head back in. "You make yourself right at home, Melody."

Melody nods again. "You're lucky," she says after Mom closes the door. "Your mom and dad are so nice."

I grin and scratch my third eye. "Most times. But when

they're cross, they turn into this two-headed screaming monster, like in a Godzilla movie. Especially Dad."

Melody smiles. "You're so lucky to have your dad."

I put my thumbnail in my mouth and start nibbling. "Hmmm ..."

"My dad ... um ... my dad, well ..." She twists her hair around one finger. "Well ... he died," she says finally. "Four years ago."

I stare at the skinny reflection of her back in my window with my good eye. Try to swallow the fat lump of sad in my throat.

Mom telling me about Melody's dad wasn't near as sad as Melody telling me.

Died ...

DIED ...

The Breath Grabber muckles onto me, makes me dizzy. No wonder Melody reminds me of *Bambi*, the saddest movie in the world.

"How?" I blurt out. "I mean, how did he ... did he ...?"

"It was an accident." She blinks a bunch of times, then smiles. "He looked like Elvis—sang like him, too." Her voice's so small, I can't hardly hear her.

My own voice, when I finally push it out, sounds like I'm talking under water. "My dad likes to sing and play the guitar." I clear my throat. "But he doesn't look like Elvis— not enough hair."

"I feel stupid for making such a fuss," Melody says. "It was the ... it sounds so dumb ... but it was the closet."

I pile up the pillows on my own bed and lean back on my elbows. "I'm scared of the dark, too. I always used to check my closet and fly onto my bed from the doorway. In case an escaped murderer or a ghost was hiding there, waiting to grab at my ankles. Still leave my closet door open at night, especially now with the new prison. Better to see the enemy coming! That's what Nanny says."

Melody giggles, but she's biting her lip like she's trying not to cry. So I keep talking.

"Is it some kind of boogie man made you scared? Like the Breath Grabber at the bottom of the swimming pool?" I stand up on my bed, plug my nose, shut my eyes, then jump down on the floor and make like I'm drowning. "Blub ... blub ... blub!"

I swim up through the air to my bed and sit back down. "At least I got my pre-beginner badge this summer."

She gives me a sad smile. "It's not exactly the boogie man. It's a true story, not a made-up one." She stands up and gets her little pouch from the dresser, then flops back down on top of the covers on my extra bed. Doesn't say anything.

I look out the corner of my eye. Her eyes are wide open and staring up at the ceiling, not even blinking. After a few minutes, she rolls over on her side.

"Jenn's a nice name," she says. "My dad calls ... called ... me Mel."

"There's a man at the Fina gas station named Mel. Short for Melvin, though."

Melody smiles and starts twisting her hair again. "Have

you ever been locked in a closet? On purpose, not for fun?"

I shake my head, only the shaking turns into a pee shiver. "Not on purpose, but I still have nightmares about the time I locked myself in the dark little bathroom by the goldfish tanks at the back of Stedman's 5¢ to $1 store. Screamed blue murder for about six hours until some man finally came with a key and rescued me." I sit up on the edge of my bed and cross my legs.

"Where I went to school before, the Residential School? The teachers locked some kids in the closet under the stairs."

"What? Why would they do that? Was it like a game?"

"Maybe for them, but it wasn't a very fun one for us. Kids got put in for trying to run away, talking our language, peeing the bed, laughing too hard." Melody lifts herself up onto one elbow, leans her cheek on her hand, and looks up from under her long eyelashes at me. She looks ashamed, like she just let a big noisy stinker during one of Reverend Dalrymple's Sunday sermons. "I lived there for two years. After my dad ... after he ... died. He lived at the same school when he was small. Same as my mom."

I stare back at her. She had to live at that horrible school and not ever go home? Only Nanny said it was the kids that were bad. Sounds to me like it was the teachers. I pick Cheeky up and chew on his banana. When it squeaks, we look at each other and giggle.

"Did Jimmy go to that school, too?"

She nods. "For a couple of years. But they sent him down

to the School for Boys after he tried to run away. It's like a prison for kids."

I shiver. "Kids can go to prison?"

She nods. "Well, it's not exactly a prison."

"Guess living in a coal cave's better than that," I say.

Melody lies back down and rubs the little pouch between her fingers. "All the teachers here are nice. Especially Miss Dill—she's so friendly."

"But why did you have to live at that nasty school?" I ask.

"Because I'm a Micmac person. But the teachers wanted to teach us to be like white people. Before my dad went ... before he passed, we lived with my parents on the Millbrook Reserve. After, we had to go to the Res School. But we got to visit Mom in the summers."

Melody stops talking and stares at me without blinking for about an hour. Gives me the willies. Looks like she's staring right through me, at something behind me on the wall. Is it her father's ghost? But I don't believe in ghosts.

I chew on my fingernails. After about an hour, I get a stitch in my throat, like the stitches I get in my belly from too much fast running, only this one's from too much sad thinking.

When Melody rolls back over, I say, "Goodnight, Mel." She doesn't say anything back, so I sit up and get rid of my throat stitch with two oatmeal cookies and a glass of grape Kool-Aid. It's my favorite but it tastes bad tonight, like Mom forgot to put in the sugar.

Mom and Dad come to tuck me in on their way to bed.

We don't talk much because Melody's moving around, smacking her lips and mumbling in her sleep. Sounds like me when I'm scared and my voice is drowning in tears. I give them an extra-long bedtime hug. "Leave the bathroom light on, okay?" I whisper.

Right after they leave, the door creaks open. I sit up straight and peek over the edge of my tickle blanket into the darkness. "Wh ... wh ... who's there?" Instead of a ghost, Skippy click-clacks across the floor. My heart settles back down and I grin and pat my bed. "Here, Skippy. Did they forget you? Come on up, boy." He jumps up and I pull his soft warm furriness down next to me. "Now, isn't this heaps better than the back porch?" He licks my face. "Mom won't mind you sleeping with me, just this once." I whisper-sing "Puff" into one soft, floppy ear, then say my prayers. "Now I lay me down to sleep, I ask thee, Lord, my soul to keep. If I should die before I wake, I ask the Lord my soul to take. God bless Mom and Dad, Bethy and Nanny and Skippy... and Melody."

Right before I fall asleep, I remember that I forgot all about the chickenpox.

CHAPTER 16

(WHEREIN Nanny Cries)

I *pound on the black wooden door with both fists. "Let me out—somebody, anybody! Let me out—it's dark in here!" Something white and feathery wisps past my cheek. Feels like there's somebody in the room, but I know I'm alone. A radio's playing somewhere. "Are You Lonesome Tonight?" ... Then it happens again, like a damp foggy breeze brushing my cheek. I jump back. "Ahhh! Who's there?" I shiver and rub my arms, then sit down and scooch back into a corner so I can see all four walls of the closet. The thing brushes past me again, only this time I see that it's got a face. An Elvis face that's ...*

Giggling? Skippy's woofing, like when he's got his bum up in the air bugging somebody to play. I feel around for him, but there's only a warm spot on my cozy quilt.

"No more doggy kisses," Melody whispers. "You stink!"

I rub the sleep out of my eyes and sit up. "Down, Sir Skips A Lot! Down! Bad dog." Even though I use his full name, he doesn't pay me any attention, just keeps licking Melody's face like it's an ice cream cone.

"Dad calls him 'Old Smeller,' 'cause he stinks at both ends," I say. "You ever read that book, *Old Yeller*? I won't tell you the ending, but it's real sad."

She shakes her head. "You won't tell anybody, about last night, I mean, will you?"

"Not if you don't want me to. I'm sure Sarah'll blab about it, though."

"You can just say that I got cut, okay?"

I nod. "I had the scariest dream, but I don't want to tell it before breakfast because it might come true."

Melody sits up and starts braiding her hair. I try to tuck my own bits of hair behind my ears and think of something else, but I have to ask.

"... Did you ever get locked in the closet at that bad school?"

She nods. "Two times. For wetting the bed. Had to stay in there all by myself until my panties dried. It was so freezing cold that winter, nobody wanted to get out from under the covers. Not even to go to the toilet. I held it too long."

"I peed my pants at school once, in Grade 1. Wade and Junior still razz me about it, usually when I get a hundred on a test. I want to say, 'Well, yeah, but at least I don't come to school with my epidermis showing.' Then they'd start checking their flies and gawking at me like I was talking Chinese or something."

Melody giggles. "That would be funny."

"I didn't have to stay in wet underpants, though. Mom brought me dry clothes."

She smiles. "You're lucky. My dad tried to run away from the school one spring with his two cousins, when he was ten. They got locked up for a whole week, and after they let him out of the closet, they shaved his head bald so he looked like a skinny old man."

I shiver, even though I'm toasty warm under my blankets. "I'd sure want to run away if they did that to me. Sounds like those teachers needed to read about Elnora Comstock so they could learn the Golden Rule."

She nods. "The Res School was almost as bad as jail. Only we weren't really locked up—but it felt like it because we couldn't go home. My dad never would've let them take me and Jimmy there."

"What language were you talking? In the closet yesterday?"

"My people's language. Micmac. We weren't allowed to speak it at the school. The teachers called it mumbo jumbo, same as you did. But I still remember ... some of it, at least. When I'm scared."

"Good job you came to school here. At least we get to go home at night."

"Mmmm ..."

"What's in your pouch?"

She picks it up and pulls it open. "It's my old dog, Rinty. My dad carved it for me." She passes the little wooden dog to me. Looks like a German Shepherd.

"Wow—it looks so real. Like he's about to start howling and chasing rabbits."

"My dad's real good at working with wood. He was teaching me and Jimmy how to carve, too, um ... before ... before, you know." She reaches in the pouch again, gets out a piece of folded-up paper. Opens it and holds it out to me. It's a pencil drawing of a little girl and a bigger boy, holding hands. It's so real it looks like a photograph.

"It's you," I say. "And Jimmy. Whoever did it's a real good drawer."

She smiles at the picture. "My dad. Wish I could draw like him."

"What do you want to do now? I've got some drawing paper."

She picks up my needlepoint off the dresser. "This is pretty."

"It's needlepoint. My Nanny's teaching me. Want me to show you?"

I take the frame and start pointing the needle. "Easy, huh?"

"It's neat," Melody says. "It's almost like doing beadwork. My mom and me like to do willow weaving."

"What's willow weaving?"

"We use branches. Crisscross them together." She shows

me with her fingers. "To make baskets. The red dogwood ones are my favorite."

"Must've been Jimmy gave Nanny that nice little twig basket," I say. "And Mom the birchbark bird feeder?"

She nods. "He feels bad that he has to borrow things. Leaving little presents helps him not feel guilty."

"I saw him one morning. Back in the summer, the morning our milk went missing. Only I thought I was seeing things. Want a turn?"

"Sure." Her fingers are faster than mine and, before long, the violets start looking like themselves.

After a while, Skippy jumps down off the bed and whines at my bedroom door.

I get up to let him out. "Be right back," I whisper. "I have to piddle." It's real quiet in the hallway. Usually Bethy's our alarm clock in the mornings. I tiptoe down the hall and stop outside her door. It's open a crack so I peek inside. Her crib's empty, but the green blinds are still down. The fuzzy yellow lamb I gave her last Christmas is missing off her dresser. Mom and Dad's door's wide open. Their bed's empty, too.

Except for Mom's stretchy silver watch.

Sitting smack-dab in the middle of her pillow.

She never goes anywhere without her watch.

Between my pee splashes, the sound of the phone ringing comes up through the floor register. It only rings once, then I hear Nanny's voice saying, "Good morning?" Like it's a question. Must be a wrong number; she doesn't say anything else.

All of a sudden, I'm starving. I skip back to my room. "Wanna eat? Mom doesn't let us get Cocoa Puffs or Lucky Charms, but we might have Pop Tarts." I look at the bare spot on my chest of drawers where the Laundry Fairy leaves my clean clothes. "You can borrow some of my clothes." We get dressed in a hurry, then bump our way downstairs on our bums.

We crash-land on the landing in a giggly heap. Nanny's sitting in the kitchen in Mom's wicker rocker holding our new red phone on her lap. It's beeping like an alarm clock, and the part you talk into is dangling by its long, twisty cord. Her gray hair's hanging down around her face, and she's crying—only it's like television with the sound turned down.

Our giggles fizzle out like sparklers.

I didn't know Nanny *could* cry.

I blink and swallow hard, walk down the three little stairs, then sit down at my place; Melody sits beside me in Dad's chair.

Soon as she hears us, Nanny wipes her eyes on her apron, then stands up real quick, turns around, and plugs the electric kettle into the stove. "Must've got something in my eye."

"Uh-huh," I say. Then we just sit there like statues, staring at a big orange and yellow bouquet of Chinese lanterns and black-eyed Susans on the table.

After the kettle boils, Nanny says, "Find yourself a seat in the living room, Jennifer. You go on ahead—I'll be right in." She gives Melody a jiggly smile. "Help yourself to the orange juice and Fluffs. The sugar's in that little bluebird bowl. Mind you don't spill anything."

"Thank you, Mrs. Parsons, ma'am," Melody says, but she doesn't get up.

I sit in the big square turquoise chair in the corner, the good one we use for Christmas pictures. Last Christmas we wore the Nova Scotia tartan jumpers Nanny made us. Looked like I was holding a baby doll. Bethy was only two weeks old. Nanny's making us green velvet dresses this year. Will Bethy be able to walk by then? I hope so.

I hum and try not to think about the empty beds. About Mom's watch.

When Nanny comes in, she sets her tea on the coffee table and herself on the forget-me-not footstool, right in front of me. Folds her hands together on her knees, like she's praying. She's dressed up, like she's going to church. But her nylons are rolled down around her ankles like doughnuts, and her yellow blouse is done up crooked where she missed a button. She clears her throat a couple times and looks back over her shoulder at the pinwheel stained-glass window in the front hall. Is she making a wish on it, same as I used to? Back when I thought it was magic like *Star Light, Star Bright*?

She bites her bottom lip, clears her throat, and twists up her apron. "Your little friend reminds me of somebody. Peppermint Patty—remember?"

"Uh-huh. She's real nice, too. But what's wrong, Nanny?"

I jump up and lean over the back of the couch to look out the picture window at the front porch. At the empty driveway. I hold my bad eye open with my chewed-up fingers and plunk myself back down. "Why were you crying? Where are Mom and Dad? Did they take Bethy out for a walk or a drive?"

We both look out the big picture window. A gray curtain of rain's pouring down off the porch roof like Niagara Falls. They'd never take Bethy out in that kind of weather.

Unless they had to.

"Where are they?" I repeat.

Nanny clears her throat again, then digs a Kleenex out of her sweater sleeve. "Now, just hold your horses, missy." She blows her nose.

I sit down and stuff my hands in under my legs to keep from chewing my fingers.

"They took the baby up to All Saints. In the middle of the night." She picks an invisible thread off her brown plaid skirt. "Poor little thing was having trouble breathing; seemed like she was getting the chickenpox, too." She tries to act cheerful, make it sound like they just took Bethy to the park, or the beach—only it doesn't work. Her voice gets all funny and squeaky when she says "breathing," like she's having trouble singing over her bridge.

I pull my hands out and hold up my fingers. My left thumbnail's the longest, so I stick it between my front teeth, start gnawing and thinking.

About how Bethy loves cooing to "Puff."

How she giggles when we play peek-a-boo ...

And how Mom said it would be dangerous for her to get the chickenpox.

Hot tears squeeze out of my eyeballs and my bad eye slams shut, trapping some inside.

"She's coming home soon, though," I blurt out. "In time for lunch. Right, Nanny?" I close both eyes. *Please say yes. Please say yes.*

Nanny squeezes my knee—only it's not a tickle squeeze. "I certainly hope so."

But she doesn't say yes, or when.

She doesn't say Bethy will be fine and dandy because she just got done being born.

I'm still waiting for her to say those things when she gets up from the stool instead. "Now, let's get some grub. It's going to be a busy old day around here."

Don't know why, since everybody's at the hospital, but I follow her back to the kitchen. Skippy's up on my chair with his front paws on the table, pushing a cereal bowl around with his tongue. Melody's leaning across the kitchen table, looking at the Christmas picture on the windowsill. The one where Bethy looks like a baby doll. "It's a nice picture," she says, "of your whole family."

I don't say anything. Nanny starts filling the sink with water.

"Mom's coming to get me in a few minutes. It's her day off. I'll get my stuff later." Mel scratches Skippy's ears and stares at the floor. "I hope Bethy's all right. I'll wait on the porch."

After she leaves, I don't feel much like eating or doing anything else. Nanny pins her hair up, then gets the feather duster out and starts attacking the cobwebs.

I follow her around and look at the clock every five minutes. "What time did they say they'd call again?"

"Soon as they're able." Nanny pats my head and tries to tuck my hair behind my ears. "Why don't you look at the television for a while? I'm just going to fix a pan of cheese biscuits and some chicken soup. Your mom and dad'll be hungry when they get home. Hospital food isn't fit for man nor beast at the best of times, let alone at night."

I'm hanging over the back of the couch, huffing breath pictures on the front window when Old Red finally crunches up the driveway. Dad gets out his side and walks around to open the other door for Mom and Bethy. I run to the door, then stop in the front hall and watch through the Jack Frost glass while they climb the front steps. Takes them about two hours. They look blurry and too skinny, like hungry ghosts holding hands. I butt in front of Nanny and yank the door open.

CHAPTER 17

(WHEREIN God is a Selfish Greedy Guts)

"Where is she? Where's Bethy?" I say. Same as when I play peek-a-boo with Bethy. Only then I make "where" into a big, long word.

"You didn't leave her in the smelly hospital, did you—all by herself?" I stare at Mom's blotchy red face, her pale lips and puffy brown eyes, then look away real quick. She makes her arms into a circle and pulls me into it. I press my cheek up against her old green corduroy coat and breathe in a big nose full of hospital. She hugs me hard; still feels like I might float away. Straight up into the sky, like a lost kite, blowing in the wind.

"Your sister ..." Dad's voice goes real high on the "ter" part. I rub my eye and peek up at him through my eyelashes. He gulps and his Adam's apple jiggles up and down, like he's trying to swallow a spiky porcupine of words. Or a big lump of sad. He pulls out his red polka dot hanky and wipes his eyes behind his black-rimmed glasses. Is he crying?

He gets down on his knees so he's the same size as me. I stick my fingers in my ears and close my eyes, but his words still squeeze in. "Grampy's looking after Bethy for us, now," he says. "In Heaven."

Mom sniffs and pats my head. "God's choir has ... has a ... sweet new angel voice."

I keep my eyes closed and stand perfectly still. If I move, my world will break into a million pieces. Like inside a kaleidoscope.

Sick old people are supposed to die.

Old people like Great Uncle Bernie, with his bum ticker.

Not soft, sweet little babies.

How can Bethy be in God's choir when she can't hardly talk?

My eye twitches. I push Mom away and try to rub the goose bumps off my arms. "What's that supposed to mean? Grampy doesn't even know Bethy. He doesn't know how to make her laugh. Or how to feed her or play with her. That's our job."

Dad's whiskery face tries to smile. "She has Lambie with her, Jenny."

I roll my good eye. Does he think Lambie turned real, up there in Heaven? Like the Velveteen Rabbit?

Mom sucks in some air, then moans and puts the back of

her hand over her mouth, like she's trying to stuff her sad back down inside her.

"But she's just a baby. She wasn't old or sick. Not that sick."

"Dr. Murray wasn't exactly sure, but he thinks the chickenpox got into her throat. Made it swell up so air couldn't get in. She wasn't able to breathe." Dad shakes his head. "She suffocated. Bethy was pretty tiny when she was born. I suppose her lungs weren't as well-developed as they might have been."

I sit down on the front hall steps, take a deep breath into my well-developed lungs and hold it. I get to sixty-two before I have to suck in some air.

Suffocating from chickenpox must be even worse than being squeezed by the Breath Grabber. Especially for a tiny baby.

I lay my head down on the stairs and close my eyes. Between the flashing dots inside my eyeballs, I see Bethy's little pink face. But she isn't laughing, and her mouth doesn't look like one of Nanny's rosebuds. It's wide open and she's screeching, same as the day I almost changed her diaper. Was that when she swallowed the chickenpox?

The stairs creak when Nanny comes up from the kitchen behind me, stands on the landing above my head. "There's hot chicken soup," she says. "Come and get it."

How can anybody even think about eating?

"Thanks, Ma," Dad says. "It's been a long night. I'm famished."

I squint through my eyelashes. He takes off his overcoat, then Mom holds out her arms and he pulls the sleeves off them, like she's a little kid, and hangs both coats in the closet.

I sit up straight. "Geez! How could you let that happen?" I don't mean to shout but Mom jumps. I've got a stitch in my throat again, and my bad eye's glued shut.

Dad takes my hand and pulls me up off the steps. "She didn't suffer, Jenny. Dr. Murray did everything he could."

I try to pull away from him. "Bethy isn't even big enough to talk."

"Doc Murray's been a doctor for a long time. We have to trust him." Dad takes me by the hand again. "Come on; let's get some lunch."

Mom and Nanny follow us into the kitchen. The whole morning's spinning around and around, like a stuck record in my brain.

Heaven …

Heaven …

Why doesn't somebody shut the stupid record player off and do an *Abracadabra!* on my dizziness?

Suffocated …

Suffocated …

Nanny sets a basket of biscuits in the middle of the table. Puts a steamy bowl of chicken soup down in front of me. I pick up my spoon and scoop up some rice and juice, then blow on it to cool it. Just like I do every time I eat soup. I look out the corner of my good eye at Mom and Dad. They're busy slurping soup, buttering biscuits, and fussing about funerals.

Don't talk about that, I want to yell. *What about the weather? What about Melody screaming and her horrible school?* Instead, I put a big chunk of cardboard chicken in my mouth and make myself chew it up and choke it down. Is this a movie? And I'm just watching and waiting for the happy-ending music?

I turn around and look at Bethy's empty ducky chair on the floor in the corner. Skippy's licking some Arrowroot crumbs out of the crack in the pink seat pad. Does he know they'll be his last Bethy crumbs ever?

"Where did the bouquet come from?" Mom asks.

"The thief, I suppose," Nanny says. "Helped his self to a few carrots from your garden, and left that bunch of weeds."

"I think they're pretty," Mom says. "Almost like he knew we'd need something to make us smile today."

I stand up and shove my chair back with my legs, hard, so it bangs into the blue checkered wallpaper and rattles the teapot clock. "May I please be excused?"

Dad nods. "Of course, Jenny." Their whispery voices follow me up the stairs.

I need to go to the bathroom, only I don't want to walk past Bethy's room, so I cross my legs and sit on the edge of my bed. Rub my tickle blanket back and forth across my top lip.

I jump when somebody knocks on my door. "Anybody home?" Nanny pokes her head in.

I sniff and nod. She sits down beside me on the bed. Pulls my head over onto her bony shoulder and pats my hair. Only she does it backwards so it hurts my chickenpox scabs.

"Is it my fault, Nanny? Did I murder Bethy? Will I have to live at the prison?"

She sits up straight and stops patting. "Upon my soul, Jennifer Elizabeth. Why in the name of time would it be your fault?"

"Bethy wouldn't have got the chickenpox if I didn't."

"It's the germ's fault, not yours," Nanny says. "God moves in mysterious ways."

"Still ... He's a selfish greedy-guts then, stealing Bethy from us."

She shakes her head, then rubs my knee. "Easy, Jennifer. Ours is not to wonder why."

My bottom lip starts wobbling again. I snuff back some snot, put both hands over my eyes, but the hot tears leak out between my fingers anyway.

Nanny wraps me up in her skinny arms. I wipe my nose on my sleeve. "Now, I'll n ... n ... never get to be a b ... b ... big sister. There's so many things I didn't get to tell her."

She rocks me back and forth. When the fire whistle blows, Nanny reaches across me and turns on my transistor radio. The announcer's getting ready to read the noon news. I flop back on my bed and listen.

"Early this morning, at All Saints Hospital, the passing

occurred of Beth Carol Parsons, infant daughter of Mr. and Mrs. Robert Parsons. Funeral arrangements are incomplete at this time."

When I sit up to click the radio off, a sunbeam pokes through the rainclouds. Is Bethy already a real angel up there, like in *The Littlest Angel*? Flying around up in the sky with her fluffy white wings and a golden halo?

Nanny gets up. "I'm just going to the bathroom."

"Me, too." I jump up and follow her down the hall. She lets me go first since I'm dancing around, then I sit on the edge of the tub and wait for her. I rip off two squares of toilet paper and count the tiny holes in between them.

If it's an even number, Bethy's still alive.

If it's odd ... 25, 26 ... 27.

I crumple it up and throw it in the garbage can.

After Nanny goes back downstairs, I curl up on my bed and close my eyes.

Even though going to Sunday school isn't my favorite thing, sometimes I need to talk to God. It's not exactly praying, it's more like gabbing—only nobody else in the room can hear since it's inside my head. One bad thing is, even though I keep hoping and wishing, God's never once answered me.

Can you hear me up there, King God? I always look at the ceiling and start with that, so he knows I'm trying to talk to him up there in his Kingdom. Same as always, God doesn't say a word. I expect he'd sound like the Friendly Giant if he ever did get around to answering.

How am I supposed to believe in you, when you let my baby sister die? Aren't you the guy who's supposed to love everybody, like in "God Sees the Little Sparrow Fall?" You know, the part that goes, "Because He loves the little things, I know He loves me, too." Well, if you love me, why'd you let Bethy die? She was pretty little, only it doesn't seem like you loved her that much—or maybe you loved her too much. Did you really need Bethy to come and live with you, right now? 'Cause that's not really fair; we needed her here with us, too, and ...

The words start jumbling up inside my head, and I'm just about asleep when somebody else knocks on the door. Mom looks pretty near normal, except for the pink rings around her eyes.

"Hi," she says. "How you doin', Jenny?"

I shrug. She's using her soft voice, the one that makes me gooey inside.

She sits down on the edge of my bed, crosses her ankles, and folds her hands on her lap. "I'm so sorry, Jenny."

I chew on my wobbly bottom lip. I want to tell her it's my fault, not hers, but I can't.

"It's okay, you know, to feel sad, and maybe confused, too," Mom says. "Even mad." When her voice cracks, I look up. Her eyes are all watery, but she tries to smile anyway, makes me even sadder. She stares down at her wedding rings and spins them around and around. When she was pregnant with Bethy, they were too tight to spin.

"Where is she? How do we know what it's like up in Heaven?"

Mom reaches out and takes one of my cold hands in both her strong warm ones. "No one knows for sure, Jenny." She puts on her thinking face, stares into space without blinking. Before I've got time to get impatient, she says, "We didn't know what life would be like here before we were born, and life on earth is pretty good, most times. It's probably even better in Heaven. That's where Bethy's soul is, up in Heaven. It's only her body over at Mr. Brown's."

"Her soul?"

Mom rubs my fingers, only she's real careful not to touch my sore hangnails. "You know the prayer—'Now I lay me down to sleep. I pray the Lord my soul to keep?'"

I nod. "I still say it in my head before I go to sleep."

"Well, the soul is the inside part of everybody ..."

"Like your heart and brain?" I interrupt.

She shakes her head. "No, the invisible inside part of us. The things that make us who we are. Our personalities, the things we love, our talents, the memories we've given to other people to keep in their hearts; the part of us that lives forever." She looks at the ceiling and closes her eyes. "The body is a container for our souls, a place for them to live during our time on earth."

"Same as a caterpillar's a container for a butterfly?" I ask.

Mom opens her eyes and smiles. "It's a little like that, I suppose."

"But, how could only part of you be alive?" I ask. "Like

that nasty gray snake that was still wiggling around even after Dad cut it in two with his axe?"

Mom smiles again. "Not exactly." She smiles, makes a fist and puts it on her bosom. "Bethy will always be with us, right here inside our hearts. And we'll see her again, someday."

"But, who will sing 'Puff' to her when she's sleepy?" My voice starts shaking again.

"Oh, Jenny. You can keep singing to her. She'll still be able to hear you."

I tilt my head and frown at her. "Maybe .... "

She smiles. "Heaven's not too far away. I'm sure Grampy's fixing a room up for her already."

"Does Grampy even know how to change diapers?"

"If not, I'm sure he'll learn."

"It's not fair. I didn't even get to say goodbye ..." I hug Cheeky and hum the first lines of "Puff."

Mom starts swaying and humming along, then she stops and sits up straight. "I have an idea! Would you like to sing to Bethy again, in church?"

"With a million people staring at me?" My heart starts thumping. "What if I faint again?"

"Well, I don't think there'll be quite that many people there. Hmm ... Let me think."

"Could I wear a Halloween mask? Then nobody'd know it was me."

"Maybe ... Or you could stand up in the balcony. That way you'd be close to Bethy—you wouldn't even have to look at the people. Just the backs of their heads."

I've always wanted to see how it looks, way up there, higher than everybody else in the church. "Maybe. Probably Sarah and them won't come anyway. Could I sing 'Puff'?"

Mom smiles. "That would be wonderful."

"Only I might change my mind if there's too many people."

"That won't be a problem. Maybe Dad will play the guitar for you."

She does a big gulpy swallow and looks down at the floor, but big silver teardrops are getting ready to drip anyway. She flops back onto the bed, and the tears squeeze out her eyes and roll slowly down into her pink ears.

I give her a Kleenex, then I flop down beside her and get my shoulder in under her armpit, nuzzle into her neck.

Mom hugs me, hard, for a real long time. I don't mind one bit that my hair gets all wet and sticky from her crying.

Dear Bren:

I am finally getting around to finishing this letter. You probably already know that I am an only child again. Somebody in your family dying is even worse than your best friend moving away. Sometimes God is a selfish greedy-guts. Mom wants me to sing to Bethy at her funeral. I'm already scared. I hope I don't faint again.

Your lonely friend,

Jenn

CHAPTER 18

(WHEREIN Jenn Discovers that Sad Crying
is Like Chickenpox)

After lunch on the day of the funeral, I put on my tartan jumper and white blouse, and we sit around in the living room. My last year's Sunday school shoes are pinching my toes.

Mom sits on the edge of her chair, like she might have to jump up and run a race any minute. I sing "Puff" inside my head. Dad tunes his guitar, and they talk about the food, the music, who'll come to the funeral, and everything under the sun.

Except Bethy.

Doesn't bother me a bit when it's finally time to go. Mr. Brown's long black car's the cleanest one I ever saw, inside and outside. Dad sits up front with Mr. Brown. Me, Mom, and Dad's guitar all cram into the back. Don't know how we'll ever squeeze Nanny in.

"Isn't that Melody?" Mom says, as we drive past the prison field.

I crank my neck around and look out the back window. Melody stuffs something into the old elm tree, then sprints back to the road. Just as we get to Wakeup Hill, somebody else runs out from behind an old shed and snatches something out of the tree. Looks like Melody, only it runs like a boy. Jimmy.

Mom's busy digging in her purse and doesn't see him. "Are Melody and her mom planning to come to the funeral?"

"Um... I think so," I say. "I hope so."

After we pick Nanny up, we drive past Junior Tattrie and his mother. He doesn't see me sticking my tongue out at him because of the dark windows. He's got on a white shirt with a collar, to cover up his raccoon tail tan rings, and black pants. No sign of his underwear anywhere. He's even got his hair slicked down and parted in the middle. Like he's going to church—only I never saw him, or smelled him, at St. Andrew's before.

Don't imagine God would want a bad, smelly boy like that inside his house.

Mr. Brown lets us out at a side door I never noticed before. We sit in a little wooden room off by ourselves, just beside the part where Reverend Dalrymple stands. In his whispery voice, Mr. Brown calls it "The Family Room," like it's a big secret we're in there.

Mom says hello to the cousins, aunts, and uncles, then goes to the mirror and paints on some new lipstick. Baby Pink. She blots her lips, then comes over to where I'm sitting on a flowery pink loveseat, and gives me the kiss-print Kleenex. "To help you get through the funeral," she whispers.

I don't expect that yellow kiss Kleenex is going to help my stomach any if it starts growling like always in church, so I stuff it into my jumper pocket. She sits down beside me, right next to a little wooden table with a sparkly glass bowl full of candy on it.

My teenage cousin Shane's parked on the other side of the candy bowl looking at the funeral bulletin. He's still got a big chickenpox scab in the middle of his nose. Or maybe it's a pimple.

"Hi, Shane," I say. "Is that a chickenpox on your nose? See my third eye?"

He doesn't answer me, but one of his cheeks is all bulged out, so I know he already helped himself. They're hard pink peppermints, the kind Nanny likes. They don't last as long as jawbreakers, but they're free, so I pop one in my mouth, stuff a few extra ones in my pocket, then get up and give two to Nanny.

Somebody's playing the organ, so I look out into the church. Mr. Brown's helpers in their penguin suits are coming up the aisle, carrying a small white box up to the front of the church. A small white coffin. It's shut up tight, but I know who's inside, wearing the brand new frilly pink dress and socks me and Mom picked out. Snuggling up to her yellow Lambie and *Old Mother West Wind*.

I blink hard to keep my tears tucked away behind my eyeballs. I want to look away, sit back down, only my legs have turned into logs. I try not to let on that I'm stuck and just stand there, staring up at the giant stained-glass windows that go straight up to the ceiling, even though I've stared at them a thousand times before. My favorite's a picture of Jesus with sad eyes and a blue dress. He's got a walking stick in one hand and a baby lamb in the other arm. Is he helping King God and Grampy look after Bethy?

Last night, Dad said I could go down to Brown's Funeral Home with him and take one last peek at Bethy if I wanted to. Or at least her body container. I said thank you very much, but no thank you. Thinking about that shiny clean coffin about to be buried deep underground in just a little while, down with all that smelly, black, dusty coal and the slimy brown worms and hairy centipedes, makes my heart start pounding.

The more I think about breathing, the harder it gets to find some air. I want to run out there and lift up the lid. Make sure Bethy's not really holding her breath, trying to trick us. My mind keeps shouting, *DO IT! DO IT!*

But I don't.

I yank my heavy feet up off the floor, clomp back to my chair and stuff another pink peppermint in my mouth. I can already feel a canker sore starting on the inside of my left cheek.

The organ plays for about an hour, then Reverend Dalrymple talks for another hour, with his rumbly Papa Bear voice that puts you to sleep. The choir's full of old people. Maybe that's why they don't use the upstairs choir loft much. When they do "God Sees the Little Sparrow Fall," Miss Dill sings like she's doing a solo in the Music Festival.

Nobody talks much about Bethy. Guess she wasn't here long enough to have many stories. She didn't even get to have a friend. I cry for a bit, mostly because Mom and Dad are, but they're trying not to.

Finally, Reverend Dalrymple smiles in at us. "Beth's sister would like to share a gift of music with us now." He folds his hands in front of him. "This is not a song frequently heard at funeral services, but it is a ballad about love and loss."

I stand up, clear my throat, and follow Dad and his guitar down the steps into the main part of the church. We tiptoe up the aisle to the back. Only it sounds like we're tap-dancing. I stare at the floor and whisper, "The lips, the teeth, the tip of the tongue." The aisle's almost as long as the one at the Music Festival church.

I count the wooden stairs up to the choir loft. "... Twenty-one, twenty-two, twenty-three. The tip of the tongue, the lips, the teeth." When we finally get there, I lift up my chin and look out over top of everybody, at the windows on the front wall. The one with Jesus and the baby lamb. I close my eyes and take ten deep breaths, real slow, just like Miss Dill tells us. *One ... one thousand ... two ... two thousand ...*

When Dad strums the first notes, I stare straight ahead,

fold my hands in front of me, then open my lips to make the words. Only I don't hear anything. I rub my frozen throat, lick my lips, then close my eyes again. When I open them this time, Miss Dill's looking right up at me. Her lips are pressed together, and she's doing a "*P-p-p-p.*"

Dad reaches out, squeezes my hand, then starts back at the beginning.

I look straight ahead.

At the picture of Jesus.

At the fuzzy little lamb.

All of a sudden, the big sore hole in my heart, where Bethy used to be, just starts leaking. Big salty tears pour down my cheeks, drip onto my blouse. I swallow hard, ball my hands up into fists, and rub my eyes. Dad stops playing and sets down his guitar. Pulls me down onto his lap and presses my face into his shoulder.

"Let us pray." After the prayer, Reverend Dalrymple talks a little more, then the organ starts playing and everybody leaves. When the church is empty and quiet, Dad and me walk back down the stairs. Mom and Nanny are waiting for us. Mom looks so sorry for me that it makes me start blubbering all over again. "I ... I ... c ... c ... couldn't d ... d ... do it. I wanted to s ... s ... sing, but no words c ... c ... came out."

Mom puts her arms around me. "Shhh ... it's all right, Jenny. You'll sing to Bethy again. You'll find the right time."

We all pile back into Mr. Brown's car and drive up to the graveyard. Angry black clouds hang over the prison, like the black smoke that belches out of the battery factory.

A big hole's already cut in the soggy grass, like a bristly yellow monster mouth waiting to gobble Bethy up.

"Let us join together now in singing our dearly departed up to Heaven."

I want to put my hand up, tell Reverend Dalrymple that Bethy's already up there, except for her body container. But I don't. We all stand in a circle. I try not to look down into the hole so I won't get dizzy and fall right in. Our singing almost covers up the squeaking and scraping noises the men make putting the coffin down into the ground with ropes. I try to think of Bethy smiling and cooing on top of the clouds, instead of being trapped inside a coffin way under the ground. Like Grampy and all those other miners.

When it's time to pray, I bow my head and squint my eyes up so they look closed, only I can still see everybody's shoes through my eyelashes. There's too many people to see them all. No sign of The Queen Smirkle Bee's fancy boots.

When Reverend Dalrymple's done praying, we all pick a flower out of the bouquets to drop in on top of the coffin. I pick a daisy. Bethy would've liked making daisy chains with me and wishing on the fuzzy yellow middles. Will somebody up in Heaven have time to teach her about *Loves Me, Loves Me Not*? Before I drop the daisy into the deep hole, I squeeze a couple of yellow seeds out, blow them into the air and make a wish to King God. *Please let Bethy's soul be safe together with Grampy's. I don't want her to be scared and lonesome.*

"I'll be right there," I say when Dad tries to take my hand to walk back to the car. I need to talk to Bethy alone.

Only I can't think of anything to say.

Nothing at all.

So I sing.

"Puff the magic dragon, lived by the sea ..." My voice doesn't crack 'til I get to the part about dragons living forever, but not so little boys, only I change it to girls. I sing through the crack, which is almost like singing over the bridge. I can almost hear Bethy cooing along. On the last chorus, I do hear somebody else singing. For real. In harmony.

When they start clapping, quietly, I turn around. Two people. One of them's standing inside the fence around the prison field. When a guard yells at him, he turns and walks away. The Elvis prisoner.

The other person's leaning against a big acorn tree, looking even prettier than on TV, and grinning. But her eyes are shiny. "Beautiful, Jennifer. Your baby sister heard every word of that."

I blush. "Thanks, Annie ... I hope you're right."

"You sang from your heart. And your soul. That's a special talent not everybody has. My old pal, Althea Dill, was right— you do have the voice of an angel."

"Maybe ... only it won't cooperate when I have to sing in front of people. Or even behind them."

"I used to have that same problem." Annie puts her arm around my shoulders. "When I was your age."

I look up at her. "Really?"

She nods. "I was ten the first time I sang at the Miners' Hall Concert. My knees were knocking together so hard I had purple bruises between them after. You going to do a solo this year?"

I shake my head. "I'm too scared."

"Why don't you think about finding a duet partner? That's how I got going—with Althea. Having a friend beside you makes you stronger."

"Mmm ... maybe. That's what Miss Dill said, too."

When the first plop of dirt thumps onto the coffin behind us, I cover my ears, and we walk away.

Annie shakes my hand when we get to the car. "I look forward to hearing more from you, Miss Parsons. Give me a call if you want a few pointers sometime when I'm in town."

I grin up at her. "Really?"

She nods. "You bet."

Even though it doesn't seem right, I can't stop smiling all the way back to the church hall. The other kids there don't even try to talk to me. What are you supposed to say when somebody's baby sister dies, anyway? When the old church people hug me, they mostly smell like roses or mothballs, but a few of the men smell like horses and hay. Some of the ladies start blubbering into their teacups soon as they try to talk to me.

Guess sad crying's like chickenpox—you can catch it real easy.

First chance we get, me and Melody take our plates outside and sit on the church steps.

"You think your dad's up in Heaven?" I ask. "His soul, I mean. Mom says your soul is the most important part of you even though it's invisible. It's even more important than your brain because it lives forever."

Melody looks up at the sky and twists her hair around her finger. "Maybe. Some people say you become part of nature when you pass. Like a sparrow or a tree." She points to the top of a big oak tree. "Maybe that eagle. The eagle's good luck—it's the creature that flies closest to the face of the Creator."

"Bethy would be a dove. You know, like you said—the mourning dove, 'cause of those little cooing sounds she makes."

Melody laughs. "We might see her sometime."

"I wish." I pop a shortbread cookie into my mouth. It's the kind that melts on your tongue. "Being sad makes me feel empty inside but it's different from hungry empty. It's like somebody stuffed a stick of dynamite in my heart and there's a big sore hole where Bethy used to be."

"Mmmm ... I know how that feels." She stands up. "You still hungry?"

"Sort of. Let's go back inside." Junior Tattrie's at the long food table, busy using both hands like steam shovels to stuff his big mouth with goodies. Somehow he already got his pants dirty even though the church is the cleanest place I know, next to Nanny's house.

I poke him in the shoulder. "Those are our treats."

Melody comes up behind me.

"Are not, Blinky. What happened—cat get your tongue back there?"

"Are too ours." I squeeze myself in between him and the plate of frosted brownies he's attacking.

"Can have as many as I want." He reaches around me, stuffs two brownies in all at once, chews for a while, then opens his mouth. "Want 'em back now?" He shifts his snake eyes over to Melody. "They taste sorta *germy*."

We both stick our tongues out, right back at him.

I'm almost too tired to write to Bren when I get home, but I do.

Dear Bren:

Today at Bethy's funeral I found out that graves are very deep, almost as deep as the Breath Grabber end of the swimming pool, and that funerals are more about people crying and being sad together than the person that died. Sad crying is real easy to catch like chickenpox.

My voice wouldn't let me sing Puff at the church. But I did after everybody left the graveyard. Annie Murray said I did good. Melody and me might sing a duet at the Concert. She makes me feel brave, same as you used to.

I miss Bethy and I miss you too. I wonder if you can write letters to people up in Heaven ...

Your lonely friend,

Jenn

CHAPTER 19

(WHEREIN Jenn and Mel Become Sisters)

Sunday night, the letter's still sitting on my orange crate. We got a sympathy card in the mail from Bren's parents, a real fancy one, with a picture of a baby angel holding a white lamb—only the lamb's face looked like Wile E. Coyote. Bren didn't even sign her own name.

When Dad comes to tuck me in, he can't stop yawning. And he smells like Old Spice and smoke. Even though he writes on the calendar every year that he quit smoking on May 26, 1965.

"You okay?" he asks.

I rub the tip of my nose but the sneeze comes anyway, then I yawn back. "Sleepy. You okay?"

He tries to smile. "I miss her." He kisses me on the forehead, then hugs my head up against his shirt. The ballpoint pen he's got in his pocket almost pokes me in the eye. "Good night, Jenny."

I snuggle Cheeky and watch him walk to the door. "Dad?"

He turns back around.

"Will I be an only child forever and ever? Not counting Skippy, I mean?"

His face crumples up. His shoulders sink, and he presses his cheek up against the edge of the door. "Sure hope not." He comes back over and hugs me. "You'd be such a wonderful big sister."

I get the prickly-tears feeling in my nose. "I miss her, too," I mumble into his shoulder. "I'm scared to go back to school. I'm all mushy inside, like a rotten banana. What if I start crying when Junior's mean to me?"

He lets me go, then wags his pointer finger at me. "*Out of life's school of war, what does not destroy me, makes me stronger.* A wise man by the name of Nietzsche once said that."

"What's it supposed to mean?"

"Learning to cope with problems is part of life, and we learn something, grow stronger, with every problem we overcome. Of course, we'll always miss Bethy, but *this too shall pass.*" He winks at me, then stands up. "That's from a Bible story."

"I hope that wise man is right. Good night, Dad."

"Sleep tight, Jenny."

Like every night after he leaves my room, Bethy's door creaks open, then shuts again real quick. I imagine he keeps wishing for magic so she'll be there in her crib again, cooing and smelling like baby powder, instead of up in Heaven with Grampy, being a soul angel in God's choir.

Melody looks pretty happy to see me at school Monday morning, but Sarah starts buzzing behind her hand to the other bees soon as I walk in the door. I try not to pay them any attention while Miss Creelman catches me up on all the work I missed.

At recess, Mel and me go downstairs to ask Miss Dill if she's got the music for the Springhill song.

She claps her hands. "Yes! I just got the sheet music for it yesterday! Wouldn't it make a lovely duet? Is that why you're asking—I hope?"

I nod. "We thought we'd learn it, for the Concert, I mean. Annie told me she used to sing duets with you."

Miss Dill smiles and looks out the window. "Ah, yes, a long time ago. Now, here's a copy of the words. There's lots of room for harmony in that song. If you'd like, I can help you practice during lunch hours."

Melody grins at her. "That'd be real nice."

When we get back to class, Junior looks up from where he's doodling on his desk with a pen. After I sit down, he reaches across and pokes me in the shoulder with it. His eyes are all slitty, same as a cobra. "Hey, Jennifer. Gotta pencil for me?"

What's he do with his own pencils? Use them to pick his nose? I unzip my red plaid pencil case, root around in the bottom, then toss him my stubbiest one, left over from last year.

Instead of thanks, he says, "You turned into an Indian lover?"

My face burns. I put my head down and stare at my math book, pretend I'm deaf.

"Wade said he seen Pocahontas over at your place all last week. She give your dog fleas?"

"Good one, Junior," Wade says.

Sarah and Penny giggle.

The *thwip* hits my ears just before the first slimy spitball pings into my cheek. I brush it off and plop my head down on my arms. When I feel another one ping off my hair, an angry red snake crawls up my chest, into my cheeks. Stops me from thinking about crying. I twist around, then stand up on my knees on my seat.

Junior's busy trying to hide his pig-ear smile behind his dirty hands. Looks like he's booger mining at the same time. The red and white striped paper straw's crumpled up on the floor by his ripped-up sneakers.

"You musta' really missed me, Junior. I missed you too— like I miss having the chickenpox up inside my nose."

His snake eyes bug open, then he turns red as a ripe tomato. Wade takes to laughing, until Junior cuffs him up the side of his head.

"It true you killed your baby sister?" Junior says. "You goin' to prison, Blinky?"

My eye doesn't even take time to twitch.

It slams shut.

I drop back down in my seat, blink fast, and pretend I'm digging for something in the drawer underneath my desk.

"You okay?" Melody whispers.

I nod, clear my throat, do a couple of big swallows.

"Maybe it was your Indian friend killed her." Junior pokes me in the shoulder again. "Melody Silly Boy *Germs*—huh ... huh?"

I don't look up. "Your epidermis is showing again," I say loudly to his sneakers. "You'd best tuck that in before everybody sees."

He zips up his fly, then makes a big commotion tucking his shirt back into his underwear.

Melody giggles behind her hands.

I sit up straight and put up my hand.

"What do you think you're doing, tattletale?" Junior whispers. "Put your stupid hand down."

"Yes, Jennifer?"

"May I please change seats, Miss Creelman?"

She glares at Junior. "We'll discuss that at lunchtime."

Every night in bed, I practice my scales, then try singing harmony to a song on the radio. Somebody named Van Morrison tonight, singing about a brown-eyed girl.

I pick up my horse chestnut twin and rub it between my fingers. It's like Melody and me. Brown and white—well, really, beige with freckles—but the colors go real good together. I curl my fingers around it, turn off my lamp, and try to sing myself to sleep. Only I can't stop being lonesome for Bethy.

I turn my lamp back on and get out my ladybug paper.

Dear Bethy:

I hope Grampy is mixing your cereal the way you like it and keeping your bum dry. Do you hear me singing Puff to you almost every day? You are the best baby sister and I miss you so much.

At least I have a friend now. It's not the same as a sister but Melody's almost as good as a sister. I hope somebody will read this to you.

Love,

Your BIG sister forever and ever,

Jenn

I put the letter in an envelope and lick the flap. Then I tiptoe down the hall and open Bethy's creaky door.

"You okay, Jenny?" Mom calls up the stairs.

"Yeah. I'm just looking for something."

I haven't been in here since ... my throat gets all tight. I blink and take a few deep breaths—of baby powder and Bethy. Now, where to put it? Her crib's still all made up, with the yellow bunny quilt Nanny made spread out on top. It smells like Ivory Snow. I hold the letter up to my cheek, then lift one corner of the quilt and tuck it in underneath.

"Sleep tight, Bethy," I whisper, then tiptoe back to my room.

Thursday after school, we walk over to Sarson's store.

"Pee—eww," Melody says. "What's that awful smell? I smelled it a few times in the summer, too."

"The slag heap," I say. "Or what some people call the clinker. Out on Lagoon Road. A mountain of garbage rocks and stuff that's left after all the coal's sifted out. Somebody set fire to it a long time ago, and nobody's ever figured out how to get it to stop burning."

"Really? Not even the firemen?"

"Yupper. Smells like rotten eggs, doesn't it? Sometimes you can't hardly see your hand in front of your face when it really gets smoking."

With the quarter Nanny gave me before she went home after the funeral, we buy a little paper bag full of penny candy, then walk back across the bridge toward the school. The clouds are just starting to spit, so we put up our hoods.

Melody points across the street. "Are we allowed to sit on The Liar's Bench?"

"Sure. If you want." I tip up my pink pixie stick and tap the rest of the strawberry powder into my mouth. "No old geezers there today."

We stand in front of the bench, and Melody traces the painted yellow letters with her finger. "Why does it say *The Liar's Bench 1942* on it?"

"The old miners like to sit here smoking and telling stories." I sit down and pat the spot beside me. "A long time ago, when Dad was little, some kids thought the old miners weren't telling the whole truth, and nothing but the truth, so they painted that sign there one night. Nobody ever bothered to paint over it."

"Don't think I'd like mine stories." Melody hugs herself, then sits down beside me. "Being closed up in the dark and all."

"We've got a picture of my Grampy sitting right here on The Liar's Bench," I say. "Before the Big Bump took him. He had a mustache like Yosemite Sam's. Can you believe somebody wrote that song about the Bump? And that it's Peter, Paul, and Mary singing it, the same ones that sing 'Puff'?"

"Sounds like they're from the Bible," Melody says.

"We're lucky Miss Dill's helping us learn it," I say. "Wanna practice?"

"Sure." She looks around. "Nobody's listening."

In the town of Springhill, you don't sleep easy.
Often the earth will tremble and groan.
When the earth is restless, miners die.
Bone and blood is the price of coal.
Bone and blood is the price of coal.

After we're done, Melody pops a pink peppermint into her mouth. "Mmm ... my mom's favorite. But won't the song make people cry?"

I dig a chocolate caramel out of the bag and unwrap

it. "Maybe. Seventy-three miners, besides my Grampy, died. More than two miles under the ground. But some of them stayed alive for days, eating coal and bark from the posts."

She makes a yuck face. "Is that one of the stories the miners made up?"

I shake my head and suck on my caramel. "Nope. That's true. It's in a book. Guess you can eat just about anything if you're hungry enough. The Draegermen never gave up on them."

"They must be really brave," she says. "The Draegermen."

The Bad Boys drive past on their bikes. Junior skids to a stop and kicks a rock in our direction.

"Seems there's been lots of stealing going on," Wade says. "Since the *Injuns* showed up."

"Just ignore them," I say to Mel. "It's sure cold today, isn't it?"

She shivers and zips up her jacket. "The man that owns our apartment didn't turn the furnace on yet. Says he's waiting for a coal delivery."

"Lots of people around here've got mines in their backyards. Bootleg mines. Like Nanny's. You're not allowed to dig up the coal because it all belongs to the company. Some of the mines are even in people's dirt-floor basements."

She giggles. "That would be handy."

"Yup. Only it gets people in trouble sometimes. This one bootlegger dug so deep into his basement floor that he went clear under the street and wound up in his neighbor's cellar woodpile!"

Her eyes pop open. "Sounds like a cartoon. The only bootleggers I ever heard tell of made moonshine."

I look up through my eyelashes. The Bad Boys are riding away. "We're just gonna stop by the cop station," Junior shouts back over his shoulder. "Tell them where to find the thief. Collect that two hundred dollar reward they're offering."

I look at Melody and we burst out laughing. "Wonder if that prisoner escaped by digging down into a mine tunnel," I say. "Like Bugs Bunny."

"Being underground would be scary." Melody shivers again. "Worse than a closet. Like being buried alive." She leans back. "Too bad you never got to sit here with your Grampy."

"Yeah. Dad's stories about keeping the money books up at the prison aren't all that exciting."

"My grandfather liked to tell stories," Melody says. "About Glooscap and his magic."

"Glooscap? Who's that?"

"A strong giant in all the Elders' stories. He was in charge of the earth—before the white man came."

"Like God?" I say. "Making the heavens and the earth?"

"Sort of. Except Glooscap was more like the son of the Creator."

"Like Jesus."

She nods. "One time he got mad at this giant beaver for

building a dam in the wrong place and flooding everything. The big muck blobs Glooscap threw at the beaver turned into the Five Islands, down the shore."

"Too bad he isn't here to throw a few muck blobs at Junior and them." I look at her and move my caramel to the other cheek with my tongue. "Is Glooscap real?"

Melody shrugs. "Maybe he used to be. But they're good stories. Especially when the Elders tell them around the fire."

"I like campfire stories," I say. "Just not the murder ones. Or the ghost ones. Even though I don't believe in ghosts." I sit on my hands. "Dad says Bethy's an angel, not a ghost."

She rubs her thumb over the little red scar on her wrist. "Your dad's so nice."

"Most times." I pull my feet up onto the bench and hug my knees. Melody does the same thing. "You still miss your dad?"

She nods, then lays her cheek on one knee. "All the time. Especially not hearing him sing around the house. He's good enough to be on the radio."

I don't know what to say after that, so we just sit there, hugging our skirts to our knees, and watching the cars splash through the mud puddles.

"I miss singing to Bethy," I say finally. "I know it's dumb, but I have nightmares that I'm gonna have to go to prison for murdering her, like Junior said. Or maybe that school Jimmy had to go to."

"But you didn't try to give her chickenpox, not on purpose."

"I know." I drop my feet to the ground. "I would hate to be locked up in prison, especially if I didn't even do anything bad."

"That happens sometimes, you know," Melody says softly. "People going to prison when they didn't do anything wrong."

I stare at her and my heart starts thumping. "Really?"

"I know somebody that happened to." She's got her face turned the other way, and she says it so quiet, I can't hardly hear her. "But it's kind of a secret."

I shrug. "I'm good at keeping secrets. I didn't tell anybody about Jimmy."

She stares at me like she's trying to figure something out, then picks a crow feather up from under the bench. "But first, we should be blood sisters."

I make a yuck face. "Blood sisters? What's that? Blood's scary."

"We both have to scratch ourselves with a feather. Then we'll rub our scratches together so our blood mixes. We'll always be part of each other."

"Same as kindred spirits? Like Anne of Green Gables and Diana Barry?"

She nods. "We can tell each other our secrets, always and forever. I'll go first."

Melody doesn't even make a face, but a line of tiny blood dots pops out on her arm soon as she scratches it. She smiles at me. "Now you."

I close my eyes, turn my hand over, and dig the feather tip into the thin skin on my wrist, only I peek to make sure I miss all the big turquoise veins. The feather's sharp on the end, but it doesn't hurt near as much as I thought.

We rub our wrists together, then hold them over our heads. Like we need to ask a question or go to the bathroom. We sit there, swinging our feet for a while, sucking on candies, and waiting for the bleeding to stop. When it does, Melody nudges me with her elbow. "Wanna hear my secret now?"

"If you want. Is it about Jimmy?"

"Not exactly." The drizzle's let up, so she pushes her hood back, tucks her hair behind her ears, and takes a deep breath.

CHAPTER 20

(WHEREIN Melody Tells the Truth on The
Liar's Bench)

But instead of talking, Melody reaches down and picks up her book bag. Pulls out a yellow folder, the kind Dad uses for work.

"That's the secret?" I say.

"Sort of." She opens the folder and starts showing me the papers inside. They're pencil drawings. Only they're so good they look like photographs. Pictures of kids, sleeping, running, playing. Deer, raccoons, and even a funny family of otters fishing in a river.

"Wow!" I say. "They look so real! Like the one your dad did of you and Jimmy holding hands. Did you draw them?"

"I wish." She shakes her head. "Remember what I said

about my dad, when I came for the sleepover?"

I look at her and nod. "Uh-huh. He died, like Elnora's father."

She looks away. "Well ... I lied." She does a big gulp. "He's not really dead."

"What?" My mouth drops open. "Not really dead?"

She twists her hair around her pointer finger. "He's why I'm here, in Springhill. He mails these to me."

"Mails them? Why doesn't he just give them to you?"

"He mails them ... well, he sends them to me ... from the prison."

"The prison?" Without me even telling it to, the right side of my mouth and cheek curls up, like when I see a garter snake wiggling in the long grass. "But why did you say he was dead, then?"

She covers her face with both hands and shakes her head. "It just seemed easier than explaining."

"Does he work up there? With Dad and Mr. Saunders and all those nasty criminals?"

"Not exactly." She hugs herself, then turns away from me and faces the school so I can barely hear what she says next. "He *is* one of those nasty criminals."

It gets real quiet after that, like somebody turned down the sound on the whole world. Except for my heart pounding in my neck, like I just ran a race. My eye starts twitching and the words burp out of me. "But why? Did he rob a bank? Steal a car?"

Melody leans forward so all her hair falls over one

shoulder. She starts braiding it. "Somebody said he did something bad—only he didn't."

"What?"

"He was driving to work one night. Some men were fighting by the side of the road ... he slowed down to see if anybody needed help. One of the men shoved another one out in front of Dad's car."

"Your dad wasn't even in the fight?"

She shakes her head. "He was trying to follow the Golden Rule. But the police said he was drunk, smelled like he took a bath in shaving lotion. The men that were fighting said my dad ran over the guy. On purpose. They were white."

Melody looks up at me with her Bambi eyes.

Like Skippy when he wants to be patted.

I stop biting my nails and put my arm through hers.

She leans her head against mine. "My dad doesn't even drink. He'd never hurt anybody."

"Geez! Did you tell them that?" I ask. "The police?"

She shakes her head. "I was only six. A little kid. Nobody cared about what I said."

"What about your mom? Didn't she tell them?"

"She tried. But they didn't believe her. Said his breath smelled like shaving lotion."

"People drink shaving lotion?" I say. "Like liquor?"

She shrugs. "No-good drunken Indian—that's what the police called him."

I suck in big deep breaths and let the air out real slow. I love the smell of Old Spice, except that it makes me sneeze.

But nobody ever accused my dad of drinking it. I close my eyes and count up to ten, then back down to zero.

I want to think of something real nice to say, but my brain's spinning like a stuck record.

Just then, Junior and Wade drive by again. Stop across from us.

"Hey—the cops are coming," Wade yells. "To arrest you—both of you!"

"Wanna play Cowboys and Indians while you're waiting?" Junior pats his mouth and does a few '*Hiya hiyas*.' "You can be the murderer Injun that pees her pants, Blinky."

"Don't even look at them, Mel. They're just showing off. Keep looking at me."

Her brown eyes stare straight at me, but it seems like she's far, far away from Springhill. Someplace safe.

A police car pulls up behind the Bad Boys. Officer Mills rolls down the window and waves to us. "Move along now, boys. Stop flirting with the girls."

I grin at Melody as the boys ride away.

"Do you get to see your dad? I mean, can you visit him up at the prison?"

"Sometimes, but not that much. They've got real strict rules for kids."

"Even stricter than the principal's rules?"

She nods. "The visits are too short. I haven't heard my dad sing in a long, long time."

I swallow hard. "Will he be in jail forever? 'Til he's an old man?"

"Not forever, but for a lot more years. At least ten." She sniffs and wipes her eyes. "I'll be a grownup by then."

I chew on my fingernails and stare at the drawings. "This one of you and Jimmy flying on the eagle's back is my favorite," I say.

"Mmmm ... Dad always told us anything was possible, even kids flying."

I close my eyes and think of Dad.

... driving us batty singing along with the radio jingles;

... making funny faces and humming when he shaves;

... being a prisoner.

When I finally look up, sparkly sunbeams pop out from behind the gray shaving-cream clouds.

"Oh! A whole rainbow," Melody says. "*Munkwon*—in my language."

I giggle. "That's a funny word. You get to make a wish. Finders keepers. First one sees it gets their wish."

"Really?"

"Yup. If it was me, I'd wish for Bethy to come back," I tell her. "Or maybe for Sarah and the Bad Boys to move to Iceland."

Melody closes her eyes. "Hmm ..." After a bit, a big smile spreads across her face. She opens her eyes again. "Am I allowed to tell you what I wished for?"

I grin. "Don't think there's any rule about that. Can if you want."

"It sounds silly ... but ... I wished ..." She sits on her hands and swings her legs back and forth under the bench. "I wished that I could hear my dad sing again ..." She presses her lips together and sniffs, then tries to smile, but only one cheek lifts up. "... I'm starting to forget how his voice sounds."

Tears prickle behind my eyeballs and my throat gets all fuzzy. Like a lost caterpillar's crawling up inside it.

When I get home, Mom's sitting at the kitchen table, looking at some pictures. Colored photographs, not black and white.

"Did you get some new pictures? From the summer?" I ask.

She takes her glasses off and looks up at me with watery eyes. "Mr. Brown brought them over. Do you want to look?"

I take them from her. They're pictures from the funeral— the flower bouquets and the little white coffin.

Mom sniffs. "I don't know what to do with them. They make me sad all over again. Every time I look at them."

"Why would he give us these stupid pictures? We need real pictures of Bethy. Ones that make us smile, not cry."

She slides them back in the envelope and presses her lips together. "You're right. I'll just put them away in a drawer. Forget about them. How about some tea and cookies?"

"Extra sugar, please," I say.

"Maybe after, you can help me take the playpen apart. We can use the extra space in the living room."

She's trying to be brave, but her lips are wobbly. "You okay, Mom?" I wrap my arms around her waist.

"I'm getting there, Jenny," she mumbles into my hair.

"I'm getting stronger, little by little." She gives me one big squeeze, then pulls away. "But it takes time. I'll plug in the kettle."

She doesn't look quite so sad when she comes to tuck me in. "When I was putting the playpen in the closet, I saw your letter," she says.

"Oh, yeah." I rub my tickle blanket against my top lip. "That."

She puts up both hands. "Don't worry. I didn't read it."

I blush. "It's kind of silly. I know that. But it made me feel better, writing it."

She smiles. "I think it's a brilliant idea. In fact, I'm thinking of keeping a diary, just for things I'd like to tell her." She hugs me. "Like what a thoughtful big sister she has ... had."

After she leaves, I get out the words Miss Dill gave us and sing the whole ballad through, three times. By the time I get to the last chorus, I can almost hear Melody singing alongside me. My belly gets all bubbly and tingly. Like the night before Christmas. When I practice my scales, my bridge doesn't seem near as high as it used to.

I sing it one more time, turn off my lamp, and pull my cozy quilt up under my chin. The moon pops out from behind my pine tree, makes everything in my room glow soft and white. Is that how it looks, way up there in Heaven?

I yawn and stare up at the ceiling. *Goodnight, Bethy*. I

smile and close my eyes, then open them and look up again. *Are you there, King God?*

I wait a few seconds, but he doesn't answer, so I keep going.

I'm sorry I called you a greedy guts, but I was sad. I'm still sad. Could you please help Melody's rainbow wish come true? And, if it's not too much trouble, if there's a girl angel that knows "Puff," could you ask her to sing to Bethy? Pretty please, with Smarties on top?

CHAPTER 21

(WHEREIN Jenn Fights Back)

Miss Dill asks us to help her wash the flutophones at lunchtime the Tuesday before the concert. Even with rubber gloves on, it's a gross job. Somehow Wade and Junior always get both mud and boogers on theirs. "I'm surprised they have any leftovers," I tell Melody. "Bits they didn't eat."

"Don't know where the time goes. Can you believe we've been working on your song for two weeks already?" Miss Dill says. "I think it'll be nice having the concert up at the new prison for a change. Help build a bridge between our communities and all that."

"Will the prisoners be able to watch?" Melody asks. She's drying and I'm washing.

"Oh, I expect so. Perhaps some of them will even perform.

But you don't need to be frightened—they'll have plenty of guards on duty."

Melody nudges me with her elbow. I nudge her back.

"Shall we practice now?"

I pull the plug to drain the water. "Are you sure people will like it? It's kind of sad. My mom cries when we practice it, but maybe it's because she's still sad about Bethy."

For a second, it looks like Miss Dill's about to cry, too, but she keeps talking instead. "It's a lovely choice. The concert is, after all, to raise funds for the Miners' Hall. And the chorus is perfect for two-part harmony. Let's warm up our voices and get to work, shall we?"

By the time the afternoon bell goes, I'm getting a frog in my throat—a bullfrog, I think—but our song sounds good.

"Your voices are sublime side by side." Miss Dill's got her hands folded together in front of her mouth and her eyes are shiny. "And, Jennifer, you're getting so close to being able to sing over your bridge. Can you come back tomorrow?"

Melody and I look at each other, giggle, and nod.

"I'm so excited the concert's going to be at the prison," Melody says as we walk back upstairs.

I smile. "Maybe you'll get to hear your dad sing."

She crosses her fingers.

"Here's the latest." Sarah's crow voice chases us across the playground at lunchtime the day before the Concert. "You know how Silly Boy hasn't got a dad?"

Melody and I stop skipping and singing and freeze.

"Yeah," Penny says. "She's half an orphan."

"You can't be half an orphan," Vickie says. "Can you?"

Sarah climbs up into the Hip Hive. "Well, don't feel sorry for her. Because she does. Have a father, I mean."

I'm listening so hard, I almost forget to breathe. My eye twitches and my insides twist up like a Slinky.

"Really?" Penny says. "Then, where is he? Are they divorced?"

"It's against the law to get divorced," Vickie says. "Isn't it?"

Wade and Junior stop their wrestling and messing around and perk up their hound dog noses.

"He's a flippin' criminal. One of the Indians up at Dad's prison."

"Whoa!" Junior says. "The one that escaped?"

"The one that's stealing everything?" Vickie asks.

"No, he's still up there. I heard My Mother talking about it. And that's not *a-a-all*." Sarah kind of sings that last part.

I look back over my shoulder. Sarah's got her arms crossed in front of her and she's giving them all her smirkle.

Melody and me push our bums into the crisscross fence and press our shoulders together. Kick some mushy brown chestnut shells in Sarah's direction.

"He's in prison for murdering somebody!"

"Did he shoot 'em with a bow and arrow?" Junior makes his hand into a gun. "Or a pistol?" He pulls the trigger. "Bang! Bang!"

"Did he give them the chickenpox, like Blinky?" Penny asks.

I squeeze my teeth together and get all hot inside ... *what does not destroy me, makes me stronger.* I make my hands into fists and rub the hard muscles in my arms.

Sarah leans forward and pretends she's whispering. Only it sounds like she's screaming into a microphone. "Ran over them with his car. Because he was *drunk*, from shaving lotion!"

"Like Old Spice?" Wade lets out a big long whistle. "Holy crapsicles!"

All five of them turn around, stare over at Melody and me.

Melody grabs hold of my jacket sleeve and tries to hold me back. My eyes, both of them, are wide open, flashing like lightning bolts, ready to jump straight out of my head and electrocute somebody. Somebody drippy like Sarah Saunders.

I shake Melody off and walk across the playground, slowly. Put my hands on my hips and try to plaster a smirkle onto my face. "Only he didn't do it."

Penny and Vickie gawk at me like I just turned into the two-headed calf at the Tatamagouche Museum. "Really?" Penny says. "You already knew?

"He wouldn't be in prison if he didn't do it." Sarah jumps down in front of me. "That place is crawling with filthy wild Indians."

"Maybe Her Royal Lowness should just mind her own beeswax," I snap back at her.

Sarah's forehead wrinkles up, same as when we do long division. She looks around at the rest of them. "Who?"

I sit on the edge of the Hip Hive, pretend I'm sucking on a cigarette, then put on a Queen voice. "Did *Mother* share that little secret with you?"

Sarah jerks back around and looks down her baby rat nose at me. Makes herself go cross-eyed. "My Mother says all Indians are good-for-nothing drunks."

I squint my eyes up and put her in an eye-lock. "How does she know? Does she even *know* any Micmac people? That's like saying all blonde people are stupid, just because you are."

The purpley-blue vein starts bouncing out of Sarah's forehead, like she's got a nasty snake squirming around inside her brain. Her lips keep opening and closing, same as a feeding guppy fish.

I jump down from the window, walk back across the playground, and take hold of Melody's arm.

Dear Bethy:

I wish somebody would send Wade and Junior to that School for Boys. They'd fit right in with the devils that work there. Sarah too, only she's a girl. Well, a girl that acts like a smelly boy.

I hope there aren't any devils, only angels up in Heaven. And that you can hear us at the Concert.

Love
Your BIG STRONG Sister,
Jenn

CHAPTER 22

(WHEREIN Melody Goes Missing)

After school, Mom gets me to try on my good white leotards. The crotch hangs down around my knees, so she gives me a pink two-dollar bill for my first pair of pantyhose. "You've got your father's long legs. Count your lucky stars somebody invented pantyhose so you don't have to fiddle around with nylons and a garter belt," she says.

"Be even luckier if I could just wear slacks all the time instead."

"Be sure to check the size—get extra small, if they have it. And bring me back the change, please."

I get my bike out of the shed and ride it down to Stedman's. The wind's shoving the gray clouds across the sky fast, and the air feels like Halloween. I try stuffing my hands up inside my jacket sleeves, but that makes them slip off the handlebars.

By the time I finish watching the goldfish and choosing between Beauty Mist and Jungle Brown, the smoke from the slag heap's hanging like pea-soup fog down the middle of Main Street. I pull my turtleneck up over my mouth and nose and pedal hard down the sidewalk. Melody's mom's standing out front of the Carlton Hotel, across from the library, in her blue prison uniform. Her arms are full of two brown paper bags of groceries, and she's peering through the smoke, up and down Main Street, like she's waiting for somebody. When she waves me over, I hop off my bike and push it across the crosswalk.

"Oh, Jennifer. I'm so glad to see you." Even with her forehead full of worry wrinkles, she's real pretty. "Were you and Melody singing today?"

I pull down my turtleneck, cough, and shake my head. "She said she was going to the library to look something up. Want me to check and see if she's still there?"

Mrs. Syliboy looks relieved. "I'll come with you. She was supposed to meet me at the Red and White, right after school."

"Probably she just forgot," I say. "That happens to me all the time."

"Jennifer Elizabeth!"

I wave at Nanny as we're crossing the street. "That's my grandmother."

Nanny's loading her groceries into the back of her truck.

"I'm just about finished letting out that j ..." Nanny stops and gives Mrs. Syliboy a funny look. "Jumper hem. Can you come out in half an hour or so to pick it up?"

"Sure. Nanny, this is Melody's mom. We're just looking for Melody."

"Pat Syliboy. Pleased to meet you." Pat smiles and sets down one bag of groceries so she can shake hands.

Nanny sticks out her hand, gives Pat a quick nod, then climbs up into her truck. "Don't forget, now."

"I won't. Maybe I'll bring Melody with me."

I lean my bike up against the library steps. Mrs. Davidson's behind the counter like always, perched on her high wooden stool. "May I help you, Jennifer?" she asks.

"Have you seen my friend, Melody? The one with the long black hair? This is her mom."

Mrs. Davidson smiles and taps her pencil against her mouse-nose mole. "Nice to meet you, Melody's mom. Such a sweet girl, and such a voracious reader! She was here right after school for about a quarter of an hour." She looks at the clock. "Can't say what time she left."

"Was she by herself?" Pat asks.

Mrs. Davidson scratches her head with the tip of the long yellow pencil, then pokes it into her gray bun. "Come to think of it, there were a few other children here. Quite a noisy bunch. More interested in horsing around than looking for books. One boy seemed very excited about finding that escaped prisoner. I had to read them the riot act. I believe they all left at about the same time."

"Who were they?" I ask.

She shakes her head. "I was busy, but I don't believe I knew their names. I'm sorry."

"Thank you." When we get outside, the streetlights are flickering on, even though it's not even suppertime.

"When I'm biking out to Nanny's, I'll keep my eyes peeled for Melody," I say.

Pat looks over top her groceries down at her wrist, pushes up her cuff with one finger so she can see her watch. "It gets dark so early now. It's just coming on to 4:30." She looks at the sky. "Feels like there's a doozey of a storm brewing."

I nod and get on my bike. "Maybe she went straight home."

She shivers. "I just have a bad feeling. Melody's always so responsible, but I'm worried she's having trouble adjusting. Especially since Jimmy ..."

My eyes bug open.

" ... got sent down to the School for Boys, then ran away."

I look back at the ground. "Um ... maybe she just got busy playing with somebody and forgot about the time."

Except I'm Melody's only friend.

But I don't tell her mom that.

"I'll head on home, then." She sets her groceries on the ground in between her feet, pulls a purple plastic rain bonnet out of her overcoat pocket, puts it on, and ties it under her chin. "Thank you, Jennifer. And I don't mean just for today." She puts her hand on mine and smiles.

I blush. "You're welcome." Then I fold the pantyhose

package in two and stuff it in my jacket pocket.

I'm just past the Miners' Monument, when a scream makes me slam on the brakes, almost run into the curb. I put my feet on the road, crank my head around. A cormorant's flapping his wings like a vampire cape, glaring down at me from the giant miner's gray cap. Like he's king of the castle. I squawk back at him, then keep going.

I wave to the old miners sitting on The Liar's Bench smoking, then turn in behind the school.

Miss Creelman's stuffing herself into her little old red car when I come around the corner to the parking lot. "Shouldn't you be home having supper?" she asks.

"I'm trying to find Melody," I say. "Her mom's worried about her."

"Oh. She's probably off reading somewhere, but if I see her, I'll tell her to go straight home." She slams the door, then rolls down the window. "All set for the concert tomorrow?"

I grin and give her a thumbs-up.

"Well, good luck finding her." She rolls up the window and starts her car. It clunks and thumps like our old wringer washer, but she eventually bumps out onto the road, toots the horn, then disappears into the slag fog.

I leave the school and drive through the smelly gray clouds to the Pit Pond, past the croaking frogs and fuzzy brown cattails, and across the bridge to Herrett Road.

Partway up Wakeup Hill, I need to stand on my pedals. The cow pasture across from the prison's empty, except for a dog barking and chasing some leaves, but there's something white in the tree. I wheel my bike through the field, stand on my tiptoes, and look inside the hollow. It's a piece of paper, school art paper, all rolled up and tied with a strip of birchbark. I pull it out and unroll it.

It's us—me and my blood sister. Sitting on The Liar's Bench. Like one of her Dad's drawings in Melody's folder. Like Mrs. Davidson's chipmunk drawing. Down in the grass part, I can just make out the letters "JS." Jimmy must be an artist, too. I turn it over. *Think somebody found me. Be careful*, is all it says. All scribbly, like he was in a hurry. I look all around, then roll it up again and put it back in the tree, push my bike out to the pavement and ride down Black River Road.

"Melody!" I holler. She's walking along the gravel shoulder, almost to Nanny's lane.

She turns around and waves. "I'm just checking on Jimmy." I stop beside her, and she climbs on behind me. "Haven't seen him since the weekend."

"I just need to pick up my jumper from Nanny," I say. "Did you see the picture Jimmy left you in the tree?"

"No. I looked but there wasn't anything there a few minutes ago."

"Oh. He must have just left it, then. It's a drawing of us, on The Liar's Bench."

When I tell her what it said, Melody's arms tighten around my middle. "Maybe he needs help. Hurry!"

"I'm pedaling as fast as I can." Nanny's lane's full of mud puddles, only they're more like The Great Lakes today. I keep my eyes on the ground and steer around them. There's fresh bike tracks in the muck. A bunch of them. Who does Nanny know besides me that rides a bike?

When we get around back of Nanny's house, she's just coming out of the barn. A gust of wind snatches the big door out of her hands and slams it back against the wall. She grabs onto it again and wrestles it closed.

"I've just gotta get my jumper, then we'll check on Jimmy," I whisper.

"Daisy and Daffy and the goats are all looked after for the night," Nanny says. "That darn calf got away from me last week. When I finally got back from tearing around the countryside hunting for him, found him tied to that paper birch tree, innocent as can be."

"Maybe he was bored," I say. "Wanted an adventure. Like a real kid."

"Humph ... he runs away again, I'll give him adventure. Starting with me chasing after him with the business end of a pitchfork. Growing like a bad weed and full of the devil he is."

"Did somebody else come visit you on a bike today?" I ask when we get inside.

She frowns at me over top her glasses. "Upon my soul— do I look like a person with friends that ride bicycles? Most everybody I know has got the arthritis or rheumatism so bad they're lucky they can walk, let alone ride a bicycle."

"Oh. We saw some tracks on the lane, but it was probably just some kids."

"Tore a strip off a couple of back-talking boys already this week for trespassing in my woods. Might have to take my twenty-two with me next time, really put the fear of God into them."

Melody gives me a nervous look.

"Is my jumper ready?"

"Just about. I've got the hem all let out—only thing is, I ran short of black thread. Thought I had plenty. I was just fixing to run back down to Stedman's." She opens the oven door. "Interested in molasses beans and brown bread?"

I pat my stomach and sniff. "Yum!"

"Give your mother a call and let her know." She jerks her head toward Melody. "She can stay, too."

"Thank you, Mrs. Parsons," Melody says.

"I'll just be two shakes of a lamb's tail." After the truck rumbles off, Nanny's big house is quiet. And cold and creaky. We call home, then I stick a little flashlight in my pocket and we follow the bike tracks, past the old stone well, up to the grassy coal cave path. Nanny's barn cat, Buttercup, follows us, then scoots ahead, chasing a saucy blue jay bouncing along the path. The church bells ringing down on Main Street sound like they're wrapped up in cotton batting. *One, two, three, four, five.*

"I'm scared," Melody whispers. "What if somebody found Jimmy and took him away? Back to the school with the devils?"

"Probably just some kids found his stuff in the cave. Let's go, but we need to be fast, before Nanny gets back."

"It was Jimmy that rescued Daffy," Melody says. "Saved him from taking a tumble into the cave. He's real good with animals."

"Maybe Nanny'd be friendlier to you if she knew that," I say.

"I don't mind. I'm used to it."

It's getting dark, and Buttercup's hard to see in the long yellow grass. "Hope she doesn't get lost out here," I say. "She mostly never leaves the barn." Brown leaves swoosh through the air. The gray sky over the prison's filling up with piles of dark lumpy clouds. I shiver and rub my arms. "Here, Buttercup. Good kitty." Thunder rolls way off in the distance.

"Let's go back," Melody whispers. "I'm scared of thunder and lightning."

A sharp crack, like a humongous shotgun blast, echoes all around us, gives me goose bumps. I clap my hands over my ears, hunch up my shoulders, and jerk my head around in that direction.

Then we see them. Leaning up against an acorn tree, close to the coal cave.

Two beat-up bikes. And the pine branches, all scattered to one side of the opening. There's no sign of Buttercup.

Flashbulb lightning explodes up over the prison, sets fire to the lumpy clouds. We hold hands and creep up to the edge of the hole.

CHAPTER 23

(WHEREIN The Coal Cave Complains)

"Buttercup!" I get down on my hands and knees. "Here, kitty, kitty ..." My voice is doing its scared shimmy shake.

"Jimmy ...?" Melody whispers at first, then gets louder. "Jimmy, are you there?" When there's still no answer, she tilts her head back. Puts her thumb knuckles up to her mouth and does a loon call. The wind carries it away, up into the sky. It gets lost in a v of honking geese heading south.

Everything's quiet after, until the wind picks up and one of Nanny's yellow and black NO TRESPASSING signs starts clattering against the trunk of a tall bushy pine tree.

Our Father who art in heaven,

hallowed be thy name.
Thy kingdom come.
Thy will be done
on earth as it is in heaven.
Give us this day our daily bread,
and forgive us our trespasses,
as we forgive those who trespass against us,
and lead us not into temptation,
but deliver us from evil …

When I'm done mumbling the words, Buttercup streaks past us into the trees. I sprint after her, with Melody racing along behind me. A low, loud rumble of thunder rolls across the sky, right on top of us. Sounds like a freight train going full tilt. When the lightning flashes, I look back over my shoulder, slam on the brakes, and spin in a circle. "Melody! Where'd you go?"

I hear crashing in the woods back a ways and take off after her. The birch trees along the edge of the graveyard look like octopus ghosts, their silvery arms waving around in the wind. The next flash of lightning splits the gray sky in two over top of the prison. I hunker down and hug my knees. Make myself into a ball so the lightning can't find me. When it's done, I get back up and run into the graveyard.

She's way ahead of me, running low through a patch of exploding dandelion fluff balls, close to the prison fence. "Melody, wait up! It's not safe... Ahhhh ...!"

I stub my toe, trip over the sharp edge of a headstone

buried in the grass. Try to catch myself with my hands, only my chin slams into the swampy ground first. My teeth slice into my lip. I groan, swallow some blood, then sit up. Rub my eyeballs to get rid of the flashing stars, sneeze, and brush the dandelion fuzz off my face.

"You okay?" Melody puffs up beside me. Looks behind me, sucks in some air and puts one hand over her mouth. Plops down on the ground next to me. "Oh!"

I twist around so I can see what she's looking at.

A little white lamb.

With Bethy underneath it. Underneath me. Or at least her body container. *Beth Carol Parsons, December 18, 1967– September 22, 1968, God's Little Sparrow.*

The prickly-tears feeling makes my nose itch. But there's no time to be sad. "Gotta get back in the woods," I say. "Too easy for the lightning to find us here."

"Storms sc ... sc ... scare me." Melody's still trying to catch her breath. "Like closets."

The thunder crashes on top of us, makes me deaf. I sneeze again, pat the lamb, and jump up, grabbing Melody's hand. "We've gotta go." I look back at the prison, or where the prison should be. Only there's nothing but darkness and fog. I pull on my ears to try and stop them from ringing.

The wind chases us back through the graveyard, whips Melody's hair around her face. She scoops it up and tucks it into the neck of her sweater, only the wind yanks it right back out. The thunder roars like a hungry lion. I bend my head down and hug myself to keep the wind from grabbing my breath. Pinecones and twigs bounce off us. Just as another bolt of lightning rips up the sky, the first big raindrops splat against us.

"What's that?" Melody screams, then drops to the ground, covers her ears and curls up in a ball. I look back to see a gigantic gray ghost of rain, howling across the prison field at us. Sounds like a million hands clapping. Only nobody's singing.

Another vicious crack of thunder booms. Then a fork of lightning crackles. Too close to us. I smell smoke at the same time as the rain slams into us, like hurricane waves at the beach.

"We've gotta hide!" I yell. "The coal cave's not far." I grab her hand and pull her up. "Come on!"

"What about Jimmy?" Melody shouts.

"Probably safe and sound in the ... what's that?" It's hard to see through the sheets of rain, but it looks like a person zigzagging through the trees ahead of us. "Is that him?"

But there's two people. They stop by the edge of the coal cave and turn around. "Blinky!" Junior shouts. "We're rich! We found the thief—in your Nanny's ..."

"Holy crapsicles!" Wade yells and looks down at his feet. "It's ..." He throws his arms up in the air, like he's walking on a balance beam; Junior grabs onto him. Then they both drop out of sight.

The bump's long when it comes, and it's powerful.

I hug onto Melody and we crouch down. The ground shudders and groans. The wind shrieks and howls. After a few seconds, a splintery sound makes me force my eyes open. The trees! I blink and squint up at them through the rain, rub my eyes. The giant prickly pines are swaying every which way, sliding and twisting like they're alive. One topples over onto another, then they both crash down.

I close my eyes again, try to stop the dizziness. Then we're sliding, too, slip-sliding on the wet grass—only it's shifting, like a giant's yanking a rug out from under us. I try to stand up, wave my arms around like I'm swimming away from the Breath Grabber. The rumbling and roaring gets louder and louder, like an underground monster's chewing up the earth under our feet. Suddenly, the ground rips apart, opens its giant soggy mouth, and I'm falling.

Like Alice down the rabbit hole.

Treading air.

Somersaulting head-over-heels.

When I finally hit the ground, I crumple up like a busted balloon. The dark swallows me whole.

I try to open my eyes, bend my fingers, wiggle my toes. Nothing works. I open my mouth to yell, but my throat's packed full of ice, and the Breath Grabber's got me.

Silence. Then voices; strong voices singing, like the men's chorus at church. Only muffled. Like they're singing at the bottom of Nanny's old stone well. I try to shake my head, tug at my ears. Struggle to push my eyelids open.

Is it God's choir?

In the town of Springhill, you don't sleep easy.
Often the earth will tremble and groan.
When the earth is restless, miners die.
Bone and blood is the price of coal.
Bone and blood is the price of coal.

And then I see them. Plain as day.

Marching up out of the mine. Draegermen and barefaced miners, all of them singing. But their faces aren't black, and their clothes aren't covered in coal dust; they're all dressed in white, even their helmets and masks, with the lamps twinkling like stars. I blink into the darkness and stare at their faces.

Nobody looks familiar.

Until I get to the very end of the row.

Underneath his bushy gray mustache, the last miner's smiling, his blue eyes sparkling, like Dad's.

And he's rocking a baby in his arms.

Even with all the singing, I can hear Bethy. Making her little cooing dove noises. Grampy holds out one hand and I struggle to get up, try to grab onto it, but I'm stuck to the coal.

Behind them, down in the bottomless mine tunnel, I see a bright light. Like the sun, only coming from deep inside the earth. Is it the Limberlost swamp turning into coal?

Then a rumbly voice, a Friendly Giant voice, says, "Are you ready to join my choir?"

I dig at my eyes and stare hard into the darkness. "Are you talking to me? Who's there?" I squint and blink, but the people are blurry. "Is that you, King God?" I shout. "No! Don't leave me alone." But the singing changes. We are climbing Jacob's ladder; we are climbing Jacob's ladder ... *And the people fade away. Until they're just silent wisps of fog, twirling across the smelly dirt floor. Grampy turns, just before he disappears. "You are strong, Jennifer. Strong and brave ..."*

I sneeze. Something soft lands on my cheek. I put my hand up to brush it away, but it clings to the back of my hand. My eyes pop open. I gasp, but I don't dare move. A beautiful pale green Luna moth's sitting on my hand, fluttering its wings, up and down, up and down, making a gentle breeze. "How did you get in here?" I whisper.

A commotion up above makes the moth flit away. Way up through the huge jagged hole in the roof of the tunnel, I see flashes of zigzag lightning stabbing through the darkness. Stones, hunks of mud and grass break free and pound down on me. Heavy, wet dirt and grass. I fold both soaked arms over top my head. Finally, the earth stops grumbling and everything goes silent. Or am I deaf? Where is everybody? I try to rub the mud out of my eyes. Pull on my ears, try and get them to work. "Mel ...?"

I've never been inside a mine before. Except for the gray light from outside, it's pitch black. And cold and musty. Like Nanny's dirt-floor cellar. There's something else: a clean smell that makes me think of Dad—only it doesn't belong here. I whisper-sing to keep myself company.

"We are climbing Jacob's Ladder; we are climbing ..."

Something scurries across in front of me, makes me dig out my flashlight, but I can't find anything with its skinny beam.

In the next flash of lightning, I stuff a scream back down inside me. Rats. Two big mine rats are gnawing on a broken post. When they see me, they disappear into the dark corners.

I hug myself and squinch my toes up inside my boots. Through the ringing in my ears, I hear something else. I straighten up, stare into the darkness, and listen hard.

Priest talk. Mumbo jumbo.

"Mel!" I get onto my hands and knees and push myself up, only I can't stand straight. Are my ribs broken? I bend over like an old lady and follow the flashlight beam through the dark. Feels like I'm being stabbed every time I have to breathe. "Ouch!" I reach up under my jacket and push gently on my ribs to see if I can feel them sticking out. "It's okay, Mel. I'm here. Keep talking so I can find you."

"I'm stuck. Buried."

I crawl the last few feet to the big pile her muffled voice is coming from, then start digging stones and muck, like Skippy. Hold my breath so it doesn't hurt to breathe, and try not to pay attention to my belly squirming from the smells of rotten eggs ... and blood. *Bone and blood is the price of coal. Bone and blood is the price of coal ...*

"Are you hurt?"

"Think my arm's b ... b ... bleeding." Melody groans. "By my elbow."

I can see her face now and a splintery post. Stabbing right through her jacket sleeve. It's soaked with blood. I stop digging.

"We need something to tie around your arm. Are you wearing knee socks?" I shine my light around the tunnel. Nothing but posts, rocks, and dirt. Then I feel a bulge in my other pocket. I unzip it and pull out the pantyhose. "Never mind."

Melody wiggles around so I can lift the post up and away and get at her elbow. I pull her jacket sleeve off carefully, then wrap the pantyhose around her arm muscle tight and tie a double knot.

Then I go back to digging at the pile over her stomach; the dirt and rocks spray out behind me. When most of it's gone, I tug on her good hand. It's cold and she's quivering like a hummingbird. She groans and sits up.

"Is that your boot down here?" I squeeze it. "Can you move your toes?"

Mel pokes one rubber boot up out of the stones and dirt, then kicks the other one up beside it. I hold her hands and she gets to her feet slowly.

I look behind us, up through the hole at the clouds. The storm's still grumbling, but the rain's let up and changed over to drizzle. Outside looks far away. The hole's deep, like the Breath Grabber end of the pool.

"How do we g ... g ... get out of here?" Mel's holding on tight to my jacket sleeve.

I try to see into the darkness with the skinny beam of my flashlight. Lots of the poles holding up the tunnel ceiling must've collapsed and snapped in the bump. I turn around in a circle. Where's the coal cave opening?

"Is there a ladder?" Mel asks.

I shake my head.

"C ... c ... can we make one?"

We walk around the tree branches and heaps of mud and grass. Mel's limping. "Don't see anything tall enough," I say.

"Help! I'm dying! Somebody help me!" Wade's voice screeches up out of the dark at us.

"I can't see anything!" Junior shouts. Then he screams, like he's being murdered. "Ahhhh! A rat just ran across my face! Help!"

I shine my light in their direction. The batteries are already getting weak. The giant Christmas tree with the NO TRESPASSING sign's hanging upside down inside the tunnel. Dangling by just a few twisty roots. The Bad Boys must be pinned to the coal wall behind it.

"Can you move?"

"No! But g ... g ... get us out of here." Is Wade crying?

"What happened?" Junior's voice is all quaky. "Is the prisoner down here, too? The thief?"

I pull on some branches, but the heavy tree won't budge. Off to one side, there's a couple of wooden coal rakes hooked together with heavy metal chains. There's a hunting knife and a hatchet in one; Jimmy must've been using the carts for cupboards. I take the hatchet and hack away at a bunch of long skinny branches on the side of the tree facing out.

"Need to get at a thicker branch to hang onto. Closer to the trunk. Careful of your bad arm, Mel. You okay to use the other one?"

Melody picks up the knife. "I think so."

When I've got an opening cleared, I wrap both hands around a solid branch. Melody uses her good arm to hold onto a branch at the skinny end. "I'll count to three. Ready? *One ... two ... three!* Pull!"

The tree moves a little, knocking us back onto our bums, but it's enough for Wade to slide out underneath the skinny end of it. His face is black with coal so you can just see the white part of his eyes. He wipes them on his sleeve, then takes hold of a branch in between us.

Before we can pull again, the root end of the tree starts ripping free from the ground overhead. "Get back!" I yell. Just in time. The whole thing, roots and all, thuds to the dirt floor with a splintery crash of breaking branches. The wind it makes blows the wet hair back from my face. The tree lands with the side we already worked on facing out.

"Ahhh! My eye got poked out!" Junior screams. "I'm bleeding. I can't see! Hurry!"

"Come on!" I shout. "Ready? *One ... two ... three!* Pull!"

This time, the whole tree comes away from the wall. Just enough so Junior can squeeze out around the end of it. His face is ripped up, but he's still got both snake eyes. He starts running around in little circles, like the Tasmanian Devil chasing Bugs Bunny. "How do we get out? Which way's the opening? The hole with the climbing rope?"

I sneeze and point to the piles of dirt filling the tunnels.

We all look up, way up, at the giant hole. Melody grabs onto my arm. "What if there's another bump?"

I walk around the big tree. "Think this is tall enough to reach the edge?"

"If Popeye was here to help us," Junior says.

"Yeah," Wade says. "Or Superman."

I close my eyes and see angel Grampy. Hear him singing. *We are climbing Jacob's Ladder ...*

"That's it!" I clap my hands. "Maybe we can drag the tree over and ..."

"I already told you," Junior says. "It's too heavy."

I rub my eyes. What did Dad say he and Grampy did? Step, push, pull ... Step, push, pull ...

"There's four of us." Melody rubs her cut arm. "Well, three and a half, at least."

"Maybe we could, umm ... maybe push it up, a little bit at a time." I hold my arm out flat, then slowly lift it on an angle. "And pull it back at the same time, closer to the hole."

"That might work. If it's tall enough," Melody says. "Trees look a lot bigger indoors."

I pick up the axe and start chopping off some more of the smaller branches. "When one side is bald ..." Wade picks up the hunting knife, starts working alongside me. "... we can spin the tree back around, drag it over, and push the smooth skinny side up ..."

Mel finishes my sentence. "... so it's leaning against the edge of the hole! That's smart—the branches that are left will be like rungs."

"That's a dumb idea." Junior snorts. "It'll take ten years and we're not strong enough."

"Shut your trap and get rid of these." Wade piles a bunch of cut branches on Junior's arms. "Jennifer *is* the smartest kid in the whole class."

I smile to myself as I hack away at the branches. Melody and Junior lug the cut ones off to one side. When we've finally got enough hacked off, we all grab onto the lopsided tree, pull it around so the top's pointing to the opening, then drag it over underneath the lowest edge of the hole.

"You guys get in under the skinny end of the flat side. Lift it up as high as you can," I say. "We'll get in front of you and take baby steps toward the thick end. Push up and pull back at the same time."

"I don't get it," Wade says.

"Like this." Melody picks up a branch. "This is the tree. Pretend my finger is us. Step ahead, push up, pull back. Step ahead, push up, pull back. See?"

Wade nods. "We can try."

"Yuck." Junior touches the trunk, then wipes his hands on his pants. "It's all sticky."

I roll my eyes at Mel. "Never mind that. We need to hurry."

"What if the tree crushes us? Can't we just yell for somebody to rescue us?" Junior says.

"Like who?" Wade gives him a cuff. "The escaped prisoner?"

"Let's go," I say. We can only move it a few inches at a time. The tree's heavy and scratchy. At first, Wade's grunting, then he starts chanting. "Step, push, PULL. Step, push, PULL." Finally, the pointy part of the tree's back outside where it belongs. The Bad Boys scramble up it ahead of us, whooping and hollering.

"Figures. At least now we know it'll hold us." I let Melody go ahead of me. Wade holds the top steady for us. The rain's stopped, and the thunder's rumbling off in the distance up past the prison. A few stars twinkle here and there in between the black clouds of night.

We all stand close together in the wet grass. I close my eyes and gulp in big mouthfuls of fresh air, like it's Orange Crush. The slag heap fog's disappeared, and the whole world smells cold and clean. The church bells chime seven o'clock, loud and clear.

All around us, the ground's ripped up and covered with fallen trees and broken branches. "Looks like there was a war," Junior says.

I sneeze. "Smells like the soldiers were wearing Old Spice." I cover my nose with my turtleneck.

"Yeah. We brought a bottle to bribe the thief, only I dropped it."

"We seen him running in the woods last week," Wade

says. "It's an Indian—found his drawings down there ... of some Indian gi ... Hey—what's that?"

We all turn and look to where Wade's pointing. At a light flickering through the trees.

"Mel! Are you okay?" Sounds like somebody's talking through a tube.

"Jimmy!" Mel runs to her brother.

He sets down the kerosene lantern, takes off the mask. Uncle Charlie's Draegerman mask from Nanny's barn. He puts his other arm around Melody. "Are you hurt?"

"Just my arm but I'll be okay. Did you hear my loon call? We couldn't find you."

"I was further down in the tunnel. Somebody found my hiding place. The earthquake almost buried me. I put on the mask in case I needed it to breathe."

As they get closer to us, Junior puts his hands up in the air and backs away. "Don't hurt me!"

Jimmy laughs ... and makes the peace sign with two fingers.

"You that escaped prisoner?" Wade says. "The Injun thief?"

Melody gives them a fierce look. "You can't tell. Promise you won't tell anybody about him."

"But the reward ..." Junior says.

"He's not the escaped prisoner," I say. "Or a thief."

Wade punches Junior in the arm. "Forget it. We're safe."

"But who the heck is he, anyway?" Junior looks at Jimmy.

"You steal that lantern? Sarah's dad'll put you in his pris ..."

I turn and stare at Junior. We all stare at him. "What? Just trying to help the cops," he says.

Nobody else says anything. When we turn back around, Jimmy's gone.

"All right. All right! I promise." Junior crosses his heart, but I'm pretty sure he's got his other fingers crossed behind his back. "My dad'd give me a lickin' if he found out I was playing around in the sinkholes anyways."

"Let's go back to Nanny's," I say. "We'll just say we were playing in the woods and the bump surprised us."

Melody laughs. "Well, the last part's true."

"Why is he a secret?" Junior asks as he pushes his bike down the path. "If he's the escaped prisoner, he should be arrested. How about we split the reward?"

"Mind your own beeswax," I say, holding onto my ribs. "And you're welcome."

Junior gives me a pig-ear grin. "For what?"

I sneeze, then glare at him.

"You'd still be stuck behind that stupid tree," Mel says, "if it wasn't for Jenn."

"Oh, that. Yeah. Thanks, Blinky."

I stop walking. "My name is Jennifer."

"Oh, yeah. Thanks, Jennifer."

"What in tarnation are you fool kids doing out in the woods in this weather?" Nanny's standing on the back porch with Buttercup, waiting for us. But she's scowling like she's none too happy to see us. When I try to hug her, she puts up both hands to stop me. "You look like chimney sweeps.

Even Buttercup had the good sense to head for home once the lightning started. Would've come looking for you, only somebody helped their self to my flashlight. Get yourselves into the back of the truck—no ifs, ands, or buts." She sniffs and pulls on her boots. "What on earth stinks to the high heavens?"

"Old Spice," I say, "but it's a long story, Nanny."

After we drop the Bad Boys and their bikes off, we head straight for All Saints. Nanny calls Mom and Pat, and they meet us in the waiting room. After the crying and the hugging's done, Mom remembers her manners.

"Oh, Nanny—have you met Melody's mom? Patricia Syliboy—meet Catherine Parsons."

"Met before, on the street," Nanny says. But she sticks her hand out anyway.

Melody's mom twists her long hair around her pointer finger. Then she takes Nanny's hand in both of hers and smiles. "Mrs. Parsnips?"

Nanny frowns, then claps both wrinkly hands over her mouth. "Upon my soul! Patty? Peppermint Patty?" Her blueberry eyes get all watery.

Mrs. Syliboy nods.

Melody looks at me and giggles.

"Well, I ... I ... Upon my soul. After all these years. I thought you looked familiar. And Melody here is your little girl?"

"Uh-huh."

"Upon my soul. Can you believe it?" Nanny shakes her

head, and we all stand there for the longest time, grinning like jack-o-lanterns, until Doc Murray shows up.

Dear Bethy:

For once I was glad you weren't here today. We had a BIG BUMP and I almost turned into an angel. I even saw you and Grampy. Did you see me? Being stuck inside a coal cave is horrible! Even though I didn't really want to, I saved the Bad Boys. I hurt my ribs but Doc Murray taped them so I can still sing. I'm sooooo... tired! And tomorrow's the Concert—I hope you'll be able to hear us.

Sleep tight, Bethy,

Your BIG BRAVE Sister,

Jenn

CHAPTER 24

(WHEREIN The Angels Sing)

We have one last practice with Miss Dill at recess Friday morning. "I'm immensely proud of you, both of you." She folds her hands together in front of her mouth. "You've worked so diligently. Truly, the heavenly voices of angels will ring out tonight!"

I look at Melody, rub the goose egg on my head, pat my taped ribs, and grin. "We're happy we're not real angels, Miss Dill," I say. "Did you hear about the bump and Nanny's coal cave?"

She nods, closes her eyes, and holds up the palms of her hands. "Try to put that dreadful experience behind you." She opens her eyes and smiles. "Eyes straight ahead, girls. We have an exciting lineup for the Concert this year."

"Thank you for helping us," Melody says.

Miss Dill hugs us both, gently, then waves us away while she's wiping her eyes. "That's what I do. It was entirely my pleasure."

After supper, I put on my white blouse and my blue tartan jumper. Even with all the commotion yesterday, Nanny still managed to get it hemmed. Mom got me new pantyhose, and I'm real careful scrunching them up over my toes and tugging them up my bony legs, so they don't get a run. They feel cool and silky, not lumpy and hot like my old leotards; my Sunday school shoes don't pinch so much, either.

I stand in front of my dresser mirror and examine my face. Even my third eye only left a tiny white chickenpox scar. My hair's long enough now to wear barrettes, so I tuck a yellow butterfly one in above each ear. Elnora would've loved them.

When we get to the prison, there's already a lineup outside the door. "Harvest moon tonight," Nanny says. "Hope there's no crazies in this bunch."

Melody saved me a seat in the front row. She's wearing a long-sleeved white blouse, to cover up her bandage, and the green jumper.

I sit down and smooth out my jumper. "I've never been to the prison before. It's not as scary as I thought."

She smiles. "There's lots of lights. And windows. Not like a closet at all."

"Do you know when we're on?"

Melody shakes her head.

By the time Miss Dill gets up to talk, every seat in the room's filled. Some of the prison people are standing in front of the tall windows along the outside wall.

"Thank you all so much for coming out to support our annual concert. The venue is different, but our usual strong sense of community spirit is here with us. We have a fabulous line-up of talent for your listening pleasure this evening, including a very special guest who will be getting our evening under way with *God Save the Queen*. Judging by the size of this crowd, I suspect the news about our surprise guest leaked out earlier today."

A few people clap, and Sarah shouts out, "Annie!"

Miss Dill holds one arm out toward backstage. "Without further ado, ladies and gentlemen, girls and boys, please welcome back, straight from the *Singalong Jubilee* stage in Halifax ... the pride of Springhill, and my good friend, Miss Anne Murray!"

She comes out from behind the curtain, wearing hip-huggers, a blue blouse, and a big smile. Looking just like she does on television, except she's real. We all stand up when Miss Dill starts playing the piano. Turn and stare at the picture of the Queen between the flags on the back wall. I stand sideways so I can still see Annie with one eye. We stay standing and clap like crazy after she's done, until Miss Dill waves for us to stop. Annie takes a bow. "Thanks, everybody, for inviting me to join you this year," she says. "I'd like to do a song now by Joni Mitchell. I'm pleased to say it'll be one of the cuts on my first record that's due out in a few weeks. Hope you like it."

Her very own record! Maybe Mom'll get it for me for Christmas. It's a song I don't know, about looking at life from both sides now, but I like it. After all the clapping's done, Annie takes a bow, then waves and jumps down off the stage. Walks right up to me. Bends down close to my ear.

"Sorry I can't stick around to hear your song," she says. "But I'm due back in Halifax. Let that angel's voice sing out!" She winks at me, then grins at Melody. "This your partner?"

I nod.

She crouches down in front of us, puts a hand on each of our shoulders. "Remember—sing with your heart and soul; harmony's a powerful thing."

Before I can think of anything to say back, she's gone, and the back doors are swinging shut behind her.

My belly's full of nervous happy bubbles straight through to intermission.

We go out in the hall, where the church ladies are serving goodies and juice. "Are you girls nervous?" Mom asks. "I sure would be."

We giggle. "Miss Dill gave us some tips about nerves," I say.

"We'll be staring at the Queen on the back wall the whole time," Melody says. "Pretending she's the only one in the room."

"And picturing everybody else naked," I add.

"Ooohhh!" Vickie buttons up her sweater. "Are you allowed to do that?"

When Miss Dill rings the bell, we all parade back into the hall.

Sarah pokes me in the leg as we're walking back to our seats. "What did Annie say to you? She tell you she's going to be my new vocal coach?"

I give her a smirkle. "No, she was just saying how much my voice sounds like hers when she was ten."

Her fish lips drop open. I smile and sit down next to Melody.

When it's our turn, Mel and me walk up the stairs on opposite sides of the stage, meet in the middle, and rub our sister scars together. Only it looks like we're slapping hands. We smile and nod at Miss Dill and she starts playing. I lick my lips, look up, and sing to the Queen. For once, my voice stays strong—it doesn't even try to chase after Melody's. Both our voices stay right where they belong. Side by side, singing perfect harmony.

In the town of Springhill, you don't sleep easy
Often the earth will tremble and groan.
When the earth is restless, miners die.
Bone and blood is the price of coal
Bone and blood is the price of coal

I don't look down at the audience until the very last note. Miss Creelman's digging a tissue out of her big purse; Mom's doing her Mr. Kool-Aid smile; and Nanny and Peppermint Patty are already clapping. Dad's doing a two-finger whistle. Then, all around them, people start standing up. Stomping their feet and clapping to beat the band. We hold hands and bow. A reporter from *The Record* takes about five pictures of us. And everybody's still clapping when we finally get back to our seats.

"I've never seen them stand up like that before," I whisper to Melody. "Must be what Annie meant about harmony being powerful."

When it's quiet again, Miss Dill goes back to the microphone. "Thank you, Melody and Jennifer. These young ladies have worked very hard toward this lovely performance tonight. Bravo!"

She clears her throat. "We have another special duet tonight. Please join me in welcoming back The Singing Miner, Mr. Maurice Ruddick, and, for the first time on the Springhill stage, Mr. Joseph Syliboy."

Melody grabs onto my hand and squeezes my fingers hard.

Mr. Ruddick comes out first and sits down on one of the tall wooden stools. Then another man comes out and picks up the guitar leaning against the other stool. The Elvis prisoner. Melody's brown eyes are shining, and she's grinning like that crazy cat in *Alice in Wonderland*. Only it looks real nice on her.

"We'd like to do a little Elvis for you tonight," Mr. Ruddick says. "I was lucky enough to find myself a partner in town that knows just about every song The King ever did. But before we get to that, my partner here would like to start us off with this one ..."

Melody's dad strums the opening chords, smiles at Melody, then starts to sing. Seems like him and Melody are the only ones in the room.

> *Amazing grace! How sweet the sound*
> *That saved a wretch like me.*
> *I once was lost, but now am found,*
> *Was blind, but now I see.*

When he starts singing the next part, Melody sings with him. For mumbo jumbo, it sounds real pretty.

> *Wleyuti tán tel-wltáq*
> *Kisi-wsîtawíik*
> *Néwt keskaiap, Niké wéjíimk*
> *Nekapikwaiap niké welapi*

The look on Mel's face gives me goose bumps. Even though she's smiling, two big tears roll down her cheeks.

After, her dad and Mr. Ruddick do a bunch of Elvis songs, but that first one is all I can really remember.

"And now, ladies and gentlemen," Miss Dill says. "For our finale this year, I've chosen a song for our school choir to sing, and I do hope you will take its heartwarming message with you, out into this cold autumn night. Thank you all so much for coming."

We get lined up on the stage, then Miss Dill starts playing. I've got a solo in the middle, but I don't even think about fainting. My voice soars up over my bridge, like an eagle. From the way Miss Dill's smiling after, I don't think she minded that I changed *brother* to *sister*.

> *Let there be peace on earth*
> *And let it begin with me.*
> *Let there be peace on earth*
> *The peace that was meant to be.*
> *With God as our father*
> *Brothers all are we.*
> *Let me walk with my sister*
> *In perfect harmony.*

When the concert's over, Mr. Saunders and one of the guards take Melody and her mom off somewhere in the prison for a family visit. Seems like they're gone an awful long time.

I wait in the front hall with Mom and Dad and Nanny. My face won't stop blushing from all the nice things people say on their way out.

Mel's eyes are wet when she finally comes back, but she's smiling. We drop Nanny off first. Nanny even lets Peppermint Patty hug her before she gets out of the car.

We're just by the split elm in the pasture across from the prison, when Mel shouts, "Stop! I mean, stop, please."

Dad pulls Old Red over to the side of the road.

"Do you have to go to the bathroom, dear?" Mom asks.

Without answering, Melody opens the door and gets out. "Come on, Mom," she says. "I've got something to show you. Something good."

"Does it have to be right now? I'm sure the Parsons are anxious to get home to bed," Pat says. "It's been a long week."

Mel takes her hand and pulls her out of the car. "Right now. It'll only take a minute."

They hold hands and walk through the long grass to the old elm tree. The full yellow moon looks like it's caught in its top branches. Mel must've decided to tell her mom before the Bad Boys got a chance to blab. Jimmy steps out from behind the tree. Throws his arms around his mom. After a few seconds, they break apart, then pull Melody into the hug, too.

"Who on earth is that?" Mom turns and looks at me.

"Can you keep a secret?"

When all the explaining's done, we drive Mel and Pat home. I'm yawning so much I can hardly keep my eyes open long enough to walk up the stairs. I snuggle up to Cheeky. My brain's spinning like a kaleidoscope. What'll happen to Jimmy? Will he have to go to prison for stealing? Will we have to go to prison for protecting him? Through my floor register, I can hear Dad talking to somebody on the phone. Isn't it kind of late to be making phone calls? When I get dizzy from too much thinking, I turn on my lamp and get out a fresh sheet of ladybug paper.

243

Dear Bethy:

Did you hear us? Me and Melody singing harmony? It's powerful, just like Annie said! I hope you're doing okay up there in God's choir. I'm worried about Jimmy and I'm worried about you too. It'd be real nice if you could send me a sign just to let me know you're all right. Just something little— pretty please with chocolate sundae sauce on top?

Your BIG SISTER for always,

Jenny

Before school in the morning, I meet Mel at The Liar's Bench.

"I've been bursting with wanting to tell you." Melody sits down and pats the spot beside her. Soon as I sit down, she pops up again, like a jack-in-the-box. "Mr. Saunders called Mom this morning, said Dad might not have to stay in prison that long after all."

I clap my hands and jump up beside her. "Geez! That's incredible!"

"He said Dad's been an exemplary prisoner, whatever that means. Teaching the other ones to draw and play guitar. He's even getting paid to do some drawings to hang up in the prison."

"That's even better than your rainbow wish." I rub my blood sister scar. "I've got news, too."

"What? Was our picture in the paper this morning?"

I sit back down and shake my head. "Even better. Dad talked to Nanny last night, after we got home. She said she'll take responsibility for Jimmy, so long as he helps her out around the farm."

"Will the school devils let her do that?"

I nod. "Dad called Officer Mills first thing this morning, and he's pretty sure it'll be okay with the people at the School for Boys since Jimmy's almost eighteen. Nanny's been wishing she had somebody to help her, and she'll even give him a little money so he can pay back the people he borrowed stuff from."

"This is like a miracle." Melody sits back down beside me. Her eyes are wet and shiny. "And can you believe Mom knew your Nanny? So long ago?"

I giggle. "Well, Nanny always says God moves in mysterious ways. Guess she's probably right."

We're still early for school, so we keep sitting on the bench, swinging our legs under it, and watching the traffic drive by.

In between cars, I put one hand behind my ear and squint up at the sky. "What's that?"

She tilts her head up. "I don't hear anything. Just the cars."

"No, wait 'til that car's gone. Is it an owl? Or a pigeon?"

Melody looks up at the roof of the school. Then she points at the bare branches of the big horse chestnut tree, puts her other pointer finger to her lips and smiles. "Shhh ..."

I squint hard. It's a bird, brown and white with black freckles. Puffing out its neck and cooing. "What is it?" I whisper. "I've never seen a pretty bird like that before."

Mel turns to face me, all serious. "It's a mourning dove. Remember? The bird I said Bethy sounded like? It's a sign of peace."

The prickly-tears feeling fills my nose. "It's like how you said. People can come back, as part of nature."

"Maybe."

We stand up together, hold hands, and stare at the dove. "Does it kind of sound like 'Puff' to you?" I whisper.

Melody smiles and nods.

The dove keeps cooing for the longest time. Then it spreads its wings wide and soars straight up into the clear blue sky.

PUFF THE MAGIC DRAGON

You grew up in Truro, Nova Scotia, but you chose to set this story in the town of Springhill. Why did you make that choice?

It would have been more logical for me to set this novel in Truro, since there is a good chunk of my own childhood in the story, although it's fictionalized. I chose Springhill instead, partially because I felt that eighty kilometer distance would provide a buffer—ensure the book would be read as pure fiction, rather than an autobiographical sort of novel. Springhill worked because of the prison, which was new in 1968; because it was the home of Anne Murray, a perfect role model for Jenn; and because the mines and the bumps gave me a metaphor for the undercurrents of racism in the story.

Bullying is an issue of great concern these days among school children. How is it that the friendship between Jenn and Melody makes them stronger than the group of girls led by Sarah?

I had the same best friend (Brenda) for pretty much my

entire childhood. She was my "go-to" person, the one I could always count on, my small-but-mighty defender, and the person who typically shared my opinions about people and events. Our friendship helped me find the courage to navigate the sometimes stormy waters of childhood. Kids still seek out true, all-weather friends; the effects of such bonds, or lack thereof, we carry with us throughout our lives. In the long run, friendships founded on common beliefs, values, and interests make kids stronger, boost their self-esteem; shallow associations founded on being "cool" are more disposable and contribute less to personal growth and development. Interestingly, I have vivid memories of the children who were ostracized at my elementary school, but I can't recall the names and faces of the bullies. I was ashamed of being a silent bystander as a child, but it caused me to become a lifelong advocate for the underdog, and I'm happy to be able to write books about strong kids surviving difficult lives.

In this story, some of the adults express prejudices against Melody and the Mi'kmaq people. Why do you think children more easily set aside such prejudices than adults?

No one is born hating another person because of the color of his skin, or his background, or his religion. People must learn to hate, and if they can learn to hate, they can be taught to love, for love comes more naturally to the human heart than its opposite. This perfect quote from Nelson Mandela says it all. No one is born with prejudice—it is learned behavior. Sensitive, intelligent kids know, almost instinctively, the difference between right and wrong; they're much more flexible and accepting than adults and more likely to form opinions based on an individual's behavior, rather than disliking someone for no good reason. They're more apt to form their own opinions after getting to know a person rather than having irrational attitudes toward a certain group of people based on preconceived, and often incorrect, notions. Most children are curious and interested in finding out about people of all types—they look to find friends, not make enemies. In response to Sarah's blanket statement about all Native people being good-for-nothing, Jenn says: "That's like saying all people with blonde hair are stupid, just because you are." Jenn is wise beyond her years, in part because of her friendship with Melody.

Music is a very important part of Jenn's life throughout the story. What lies behind the choices of the songs that are part of her life?

When I was growing up, my dad was in a dance band, and he opened a music store in the basement of our house in 1967, so music was very much a part of my growing-up years. I always wished I was brave enough to be a singer—we often sang around the house, and I played the banjo for a time, but I was painfully shy as a child. I did play the piano in the local music festival, and, like Jenn, I did have my picture in the newspaper—chewing on my fingernails while waiting to play.

Song lyrics can contain some of the most incredibly profound thoughts and can provide insights into the time in which they were written. Fortunately, the 1960s provided me with a vast catalogue of music from which to choose; it seems the songs you learn when you're young are the ones you never forget, such as some of the old hymns I sang in Sunday school. I've always been an Anne Murray fan—I remember being amazed that someone from just down the road could become so famous. I didn't actually set out to include so many song references, but frequently during the writing, a perfect song would spring to mind, so I would include it. I hope some readers might take the time to look up a few of these great old songs on YouTube— I've included a list of the songs and their creators in the Acknowledgments.

This story is set in a period more than forty years ago. In what ways do you think the experiences of children today differ from the lives of Jenn and Melody?

Prejudice, of course, still exists, but it isn't as common nor as blatant as it was during the 1960s. Bullying has always been around, but it wasn't talked about then as it is now, and everyone was aware of the omnipresent "STRAP" in the principal's drawer. Kids today have the world at their fingertips, literally, and I hope that's allowing them to experience a larger world than the small one we were exposed to in rural Nova Scotia. We were so innocent and unworldly—I lived in terror of the "bad boys" in my neighborhood. Although I don't remember that they ever did anything to me personally, the mere possibility terrified me. As did the specter of death and the idea of being imprisoned. Because of media exposure, I think children today grow up faster and leave that innocence behind earlier. I feel they're emotionally tougher than I was, too, as a result of broadening their horizons at an earlier age. Is that an improvement? I'm not sure ...

In both your novels—this one and *A Hare in the Elephant's Trunk*—you have had to undertake a good deal of research. How important is research to the success of the story?

I've always loved digging for details (aka, research). It can be incredibly time-consuming, but I think it's worth it in terms of trying to making the setting as authentic as possible. I had a great time mining my memories (and those of my husband, sister, and friends) while I was writing. But my memory isn't perfectly reliable so I often had to do some fact-checking, even down to whether or not a certain cereal was actually available in 1968! The Internet is a wonderfully convenient resource, but I still find myself turning to books, as well. I hope young readers will come away from this story feeling they have a better understanding of what life was like for their parents or grandparents who grew up in the 1960s.

Some of what you are writing about comes out of your own experience as a child. How do you suggest young writers can draw from their own lives to write their stories?

I've always turned to writing as an emotional outlet, and writing this book was particularly therapeutic for me. I've carried the death of my baby sister with me for most of my life, and it was almost a relief to write this fictionalized account of that sad time. When I do school visits, students often ask how I come up with so many ideas. My response is to tell kids that their experiences will turn up again and again in their own writing, whether they've included it on purpose or not. A lot of stuff happens to everybody every day, and it's the fiction writer's job to turn seemingly insignificant events into interesting stories. Be nosy. Speculate, use your imagination—what if ...? Our individual experiences influence the voices that appear in our stories; it can't be avoided and should be embraced. The very best part of being a fiction writer is that *you* are in complete control—you may not be able to change events in your own past, but you can rewrite them in stories, and that's almost as good!

Thank you, Jan.

ACKNOWLEDGMENTS

I'm grateful to many people for their numerous and varied contributions to the writing of this book. Thank you, thank you so much, to:

My editor, Peter Carver—for taking me on as an apprentice, and for your patience and generous wise guidance in helping me sort through the throat clearing while learning my craft. And for your gentle nudges re any lurking/niggling issues. With you, I know my words are always in the best of hands.

Richard Dionne, Cheryl Chen, and everybody else on the Red Deer Press team, for your dedication in getting Jenn and Melody's story out into the world.

My mentor, Gary Blackwood, for your wisdom once again in helping me craft a novel out of a seemingly random collection of thoughts and ideas. I promise I will learn to outline.

The two women who've appeared on so many pages of my story—Nancy and Brenda, for helping keep me afloat on the stormy waters of childhood (and adulthood).

My friends, Laura Best, Karen Duncan, Tina O'Toole— are you sure we didn't know each other when we were ten?

The three wise women of Port Joli—Jackie, Jill, and Marcia, for caring and sharing.

My canine partners over the years—Skippy, Toby, Bailey, and Charlie, for listening so soulfully and looking like you understood.

My classmates at Willow Street School in Truro—we grew up together, and the seeds of this story were planted way back then.

My music teachers, Mrs. Dill and Miss Bethel, for helping me learn to appreciate music. And Anne Murray, whose music has touched the souls of so many and inspired generations of young singers.

My English teachers at C.E.C. and English professors at Acadia University, especially the late Jack Sheriff, for helping me understand the importance of setting, theme, structure, imagery, symbolism, and characterization to a novel. I'm finally starting to get it!

Don Tabor, Chief Administrative Officer of the Town of Springhill—for your enthusiasm in proudly sharing your town's history, and for telling me about the bumps, which became integral to this story.

The authors whose work I read in researching this story, especially Leonard Lerner, whose book *Miracle at Springhill* (1960) captures in such detail the Big Bump of 1958, and Isabelle Knockwood, for her book, *Out of the Depths*, which I stumbled upon in the Acadia Library one morning.

The creators of the many songs that provided the soundtrack for this story as I was writing:

"The Butterfly Ball," William Roscoe, 1802

"Jesus Loves Me, This I Know," Anna Bartlett Warner, 1860

"These Boots Are Made for Walkin'," Lee Hazlewood, 1966

"God Sees the Little Sparrow Fall," Maria Straub, 1874

"Land of the Silver Birch," traditional

"All I Have to Do is Dream," Felice and Boudleaux Bryant, 1958

"Puff the Magic Dragon," Peter Yarrow and Leonard Lipton, 1963

"Hush, Little Baby," traditional

"Happy Together," Gary Bonner and Alan Gordon, 1967

"Brown-Eyed Girl," Van Morrison, 1967

"Amazing Grace," John Newton, 1779

"Amazing Grace," Mi'kmaq translation, Dr. Bern Francis, 2001

"The Ballad of Springhill," Peggy Seeger and Ewan McColl, 1958

"We Are Climbing Jacob's Ladder," traditional

"Let There Be Peace on Earth," Sy Miller and Jill Jackson, 1955.

Canada Council for giving me a 2012 creation grant that allowed me to work full-time on this novel.

Access Copyright Foundation for giving me a grant to work on this project at the Carver/Stinson Port Joli workshop in 2011.

Other middle grade authors, from whom I've learned,

and continue to learn so, so much.

Teachers, librarians, parents, and booksellers who work tirelessly to help young people become lifelong readers.

My parents, Ada and Bob Mingo, and my grandparents, for sharing their love of books, and for teaching me how to live.

And finally, Don, Liam, and Shannon—for putting up with me and the cast of characters who regularly inhabit both my writing room and my mind. Your constant love and support make the bad times bearable, the good times great, and the impossible, possible. Love you!